Winter
Star

Happy Holidays Breanna!

2009

Love
Your VTs,
Michelle &
Belinda

Winter Star

Larry R. and Lisa Gleave Laycock

Covenant Communications, Inc.

Covenant

Cover image by David Muir © Digital Vision/Getty Images

Cover design copyrighted 2007 by Covenant Communications, Inc.
Cover design by Christina Ashby

Published by Covenant Communications, Inc.
American Fork, Utah

Printed in Canada
First Printing: October 2007

14 13 12 11 10 09 08 07   10 9 8 7 6 5 4 3 2 1

ISBN 13: 978-1-59811-421-8
ISBN 10: 1-59811-421-2

*To all wise men and women who follow the star
and find hope in Christ*

Winter Star

A Note to the Reader

Some things in life are unchangeable, permanently set in the heavens like the North Star. But like the stars that move with each passing day, we too can change through the seasons of our lives.

While we live, we possess the magnificent power to alter our life's course—the hope to better ourselves each day. That is the light of truth.

We hope, in the fullest sense of the word, that you will recognize and love *Winter Star* for what it is—a light in the darkness, heralding hope, offering forgiveness, and promising peace.

L. and L.

Prologue

"*Ready or not, I shan't be caught!*" *little Joey called loudly so Rachel could hear.*

Though Rachel was ten years his senior, she absolutely adored her little brother and, quite out of character for a teenager, would spend hours finding him in endless games of hide-and-seek. His other sisters, Angela and Christina, had neither the time nor the patience that Rachel had for Joey.

After he'd get home from kindergarten every day, Joey and his mother, Mary, would have lunch and take a little nip-nap—that's what Mary called his nap so it would sound like something fun, not forced. The family had learned early on that nobody forced Joey to do anything, but that fun could usually entice him to do most things.

In order to get him to lie down and hold still, Mary always had to promise him a few games of hide-and-seek with Rachel when he woke up. Then she would read to him about his and Rachel's favorite subjects: knights, kings, dragons, and the rescuing of medieval princesses.

"*Don't fall, little squirrel,*" *Rachel was constantly warning. Joey liked to hide in hard-to-reach places, and to do that he climbed . . . everything: the swing set, trees, the roof, and anything else he could manage. On more than one occasion, Rachel was forced to climb into precarious places to find him* and then help him to safety. *"Aren't you afraid of anything, Joey? Don't you know you scare me, rascal?"* Joey would just giggle, and Rachel would usually end up rolling on the ground with him in a tickling match. They especially enjoyed lying on the soft summer grass at night and finding the constellations. It was a hobby they avidly shared with their father, Joseph. The rare but treasured nights when he would come out and recount the stories that accompanied each constellation were the best. The three would stay for hours, talking, sharing, and finding.

Finding

Autumn 2007

I awoke early this morning at the very moment when the sky turns that wonderful color somewhere between indigo and gold—that time when starlight meets sunshine. October always visits me with nostalgia, but returning to my childhood home this way has been startling. This old house, once my home, was well used, lived in, and enjoyed. It has witnessed so much: innocent days of youth, fun, and happiness, as well as illness, dark days, and difficult family struggles. It has even seen death. The home is a simple yet elegant, castle-like grey stone structure, surrounded by rolling lawns and abutting a ravine filled with pine and oak. Growing up, I imagined it would have been very comfortable in an old English countryside setting—the places I read about in *Jane Eyre* or *Emma*.

I always treasured the backyard, which reaches to a fringe of forest bordered by a running brook. I imagined myself baroness of the entire land when I played and pretended here. The wraparound porch with stone columns has always been an inviting oasis of shade in summer, and in the winter the rooms within are cozy gathering places with their large, open wood-burning fireplaces. The symmetrical floor plan places a living room on one side of the house and a dining room on the other, separated by an ample old wooden stairway. The landing at the top of the stairs, which leads to a balcony, was the perfect place for imagining and for exploring the heavens.

The back of the home features an enormous picture window that opens the emerald green backyard forest to the dwellers within. Under the landing are the kitchen and family gathering room, both of which always welcomed even the most dedicated readers and stargazers with the sounds and smells of home-cooked meals and conversation. The bedrooms, built above the dining room and living room, include built-in window seats fitted to allow seating for readers as well as the placement of Dad's telescopes for stargazing.

Wrapped up in my memories, I keep returning to one past holiday season, almost twenty years ago. I remember that it was the year I turned forty-four. I can see and feel and even breathe what I experienced so long ago. How is this possible? Before today I wasn't even aware that these images and senses are still a part of me. But they are all here. It's miraculous, really.

"What ifs" keep tumbling through my thoughts— What if Santa hadn't left his red glove that year? What if we hadn't taken the gifts? What if Dad hadn't been there? What if we hadn't believed? And the star—what if there had been no star to guide us that night?

The stove hasn't been used for days, yet as the past re-creates itself in the present, cooling fall breezes waft the cinnamon scents of Mom's peach cobbler into the air. Images of enticing yet frightening first days of school shadow me through the house and yard. Though the closets are empty now, fun new school clothes appear in my mind—the clothes that every year replaced summer's barefoot freedom and endless games of imagination with schedules and normalcy. Like autumn's collage of warmth and cold, October thoughts piece together gold-tipped leaves on bare black branches, and memory-scraps paste themselves cleverly among the pages of my mind.

I reach for the bottom bureau drawer next to my bed, where I used to keep my old red-and-green winter robe, but, of course, neither are there—robe nor bureau. For a moment it's just me, October's silence, and my memories of past autumns and all that came before and after them. I shuffle down the narrow hallway into the kitchen, pour the cider that I brought with me into Dad's old copper teakettle, and leave it on the stove to warm. Thankfully, the electricity hasn't been disconnected. Being without heat is enough of a discomfort.

From the window above the kitchen sink, I watch night's last stars sacrifice themselves for morning's gold on the mountain peaks. All at once, I can remember every detail of my childhood holidays spent here in this home: Angela, Christina, Joey, and I returning frozen-footed and candy-coated on Halloween nights to quarrel over who got to sit on the heat vent by the TV while sampling the contents of our Trick-or-Treat bags; the huge oak table with the homemade place cards Mom always assigned us kids to make each Thanksgiving; the tiny, pink, chipped roses on Mom's white china, and the glistening crystal goblets we only used on holidays; the gloriously simple orange pierced with cloves that Santa left in our stockings every Christmas; oh, and I can't forget the Christmas Eve pajamas—always too big but ever soft and delightful.

Faintly, I hear my family's laughter and good-natured bantering over Christmas Eve games of Clue and Monopoly.

Mom struggles to stay awake—she always works so hard getting Christmas ready that she usually sleeps through most of Christmas Day. I hear my sisters, Angela and Christina, whispering, plotting how they will help each other win. I listen for Dad's denials when Joey accuses him of cheating. Little Joey, skinny, tousle-haired little Joey—always laughing, always bouncing—how we adore him. And how he loves to have fun. Fun is what motivates him, mostly *all* that motivates him, but that is acceptable since he is not only the baby of the family, but also the only boy.

I savor the taste of Mom's candied yams and home-baked rolls with real butter. For just a second, the scent of pine beneath hot tree lights steals its way into my nostrils, and somewhere deep inside me it awakens my childhood beliefs that life lasts forever, and that families are always together, during the holidays, secure in one another's love.

The happiness and wonder of past holidays often fleetingly capture my mind and sometimes interrupt my sleep, as they did last night and this morning, but never like this, not so completely. It's this house. Or is it my age? After sixty years, I've finally lived enough life to recognize the miracle—the marvelous, magical miracle that Santa left for our family that Christmas. Actually, I've always known it was a miracle, but I've never fully understood it—until now. With each passing year, I see more clearly what a precious gift our star led us to on that Christmas Eve so long ago. Perhaps I can finally be called one of the wise who chose to follow the star.

The sky explodes into brilliant white. The stars are gone, and the sun, surrounded with perfectly definable rays, emerges in glory. I bustle to the kitchen window near the dining table to see the sunrise from a different place, curious how changed it all is from here . . . perspective is everything. From this side, clouds block the rays and all that was white from the other side is pink.

Two squirrels knowingly appear in the backyard oak tree. They are playing . . . at least the little one is playing. I wonder if they are related . . . yes, siblings, maybe. The sun leaves the pink clouds, and the larger squirrel stops to pay tribute to the beauty. The skinny squirrel, which I'll call Joey, hops up and down, turns two summersaults, and scurries small circles around the bigger one, which I'll call Rachel. Then, nearly falling off the branch, Joey drops his acorn. Without a moment's hesitation, Rachel darts dangerously down the rope swing. She leaps down the trunk of the grand oak tree, tightropes across the decrepit garden shed, tiptoes down its side, and retrieves the lost acorn. Then she braves the same dangers in reverse order just to return the acorn to its owner. She nudges him gently as he recklessly plays his way along the narrow branches toward his knothole storehouse.

The two squirrels scamper into my memories, and I rest at the table to replay a lifetime of holidays in my mind. I stare out of the huge dining room window and meander back to the window above the kitchen sink. Watching the sun replace the stars illuminates a glorious truth for me. That's the miracle of truth—it's never new. It simply lights itself in various ways until we finally see it. Like Rocky Mountain Octobers that close the summer and paint dying leaves for Halloween spooks to crunch underfoot. And November harvests that glean glowing gold and garden grandeur for Thanksgiving. And wondrous winter stars that eternally offer light to lead the wise to Christmas. Life happens that way—always. What a miracle!

The frosty, early-morning air wafts across my legs, and I know I need to get dressed before the others arrive. It's hard for me to admit that Dad is really gone, and that this old house will soon leave our family to become the memory mill of others, but I know what has to be done. Today we will finish packing everything we're planning to keep, and tomorrow we'll hold a gigantic garage sale, and say good-bye to everything here . . . nearly every earthly possession Mom and Dad ever owned. Good-bye little worn-out brown sofa. Good-bye old scratchy green rocking chair. So long dear brass bed painted white to match the antique furniture in my little bedroom. "You can't take it with you," echoes in my mind and means more to me than it ever has before.

Dad outlived Mom by twenty years. He changed so much after Mom died. He became incredibly more open and loving. Oh, I wish she had been here to witness his marvelous metamorphosis. In fact, I hope she recognizes him when they meet in heaven! Amazingly enough, he was able to take care of himself all that time and stay right here in his home until one day two weeks ago. He got up, made his bed, dressed himself in his favorite plaid button-up, Wranglers, and cowboy boots, and then quietly lay down on the yellow bedspread. He went to sleep, and that's how we found him that afternoon when we came to visit. What a good man and father he became—maybe not perfect, but then who is?

The icy shower freezes my thoughts, and I dress snugly in my old blue sweater and jeans. The furnace is off, but being dressed and moving about warm me. The warm cider helps, too.

I move slowly, all the time learning more about life and what's important and what isn't. Then I see Dad's prized telescope in the corner of his office. It stands gracefully by the little window next to his black leather chair. The precious telescope is tarnished from age and covered in fingerprints. Dad always asked us not to clean it. That messed it up, he said. I sit down and look through it. Not much to see in the daylight, but Dad's telescope is definitely *not* going in the garage sale.

"I hope no one else wants this. It's such a part of Dad and what he was and will always be to me . . . Why am I talking out loud?" I'd like to keep it for myself, but my stomach flops. Everyone else will want it too, I realize. How will we ever decide who will get to keep it? For that matter, how will we decide who will get to keep anything deemed precious in this house?

I know Dad hasn't made a will. We tried to get him to, but he said he thought that was a bunch of bunk; he said that making wills just made the lawyers rich and that he intended to wear out all his possessions before he was through. So I didn't push it. For a minute, I remember the "you can't take it with you" idea and realize that I don't need his telescope to remember Dad and the great times he and I spent visiting while we searched the stars. I don't need it to remind me how great Dad learned to be with my kids, how he spent time with little Paul and taught him to explore the night sky. My own telescopes are far more expensive and powerful than Dad's, and I don't need this one. But on the other hand, I'd love to have it just to look at it . . . and treasure it.

I glance at the belly of the scope and notice something red. Tugging carefully on it, I discover a small red glove taped to the underside of the telescope. Inside the glove I find a white paper rolled into a neat scroll. Black writing spells my name on the outside of the scroll, and red yarn tied in a tight bow holds the scroll together. The writing is shaky, but I instantly recognize it as Dad's. I turn it over in my hand twice and then carefully untie the yarn.

To my dear Rachel,

I have taught you that the North Star is the only star that never changes its position as the earth turns. Even with the change of the seasons, it never moves. Polaris has never failed me. On more than one occasion, while hunting in the vast expanses of the Rocky Mountains, I found myself lost. But I learned that if I was patient and waited for the stars, I could always count on Polaris to lead me home . . . always.

You, my dear daughter, are my Polaris. After your mother died, and we lost Joey, I gave up hope. But you remained constant, never losing your light of hope. You never stopped believing. You believed even when I thought there was nothing left to believe. You stayed constant in your hope and your love. You guided us home.

Our stargazing times have been among the most precious moments in my life, and finding the heavens with you has been a great journey for which I am eternally grateful. Following our star and finding "Orion" are truly modern-day miracles.

Please, Rachel, I would like you to write about our searching. From the time you were small, you have had a gift . . . a creative imagination and a beautiful way with words. Explain what has happened to us, and invite those who have ears to hear and eyes to see to join our journey. Tell them how we learned to change, to keep believing, to keep trying, and to keep hoping. Remind them to always have hope, because we know that change is always possible.

My days on earth as a mortal man are few, but I want you to know that throughout eternity, I will remember our journey. Because of you, I now go to meet God with great hope. I have changed and hopefully bettered myself through the lessons I have learned on our journey.

I now hope to be reunited with your mother. I hope to hold her again and to tell her, much better than I did in life, that I love her, that I adore her. I hope, in the distant future, to laugh and play once again with my children and grandchildren in another place, at another time, as a better man. And I hope to one day join you and Peter on more star-following adventures.

Thank you, my dear daughter. Thank you for teaching me what it means to hope. My telescope is for you to keep. Though you have the means to possess better ones, I hope this one will serve to remind you of my eternal love and admiration for you.

Love Forever,

Dad

"Thank you, Daddy. I love you. Thank you . . . not for leaving your telescope to me, but for remembering what I am remembering today, and for sharing yourself and your delightful stargazing with me." I scan the room as I wipe my eyes. Tiny red gloves holding similar notes for other family members appear on and beneath several precious objects in the room. Smiling, I walk through the rest of the house and find red gloves everywhere.

I hold my note close to my lips and kiss it softly. "I will always love you, Daddy. Thank you for allowing me to find you. Thank you for teaching me to follow the star. We learned it together, didn't we? Change is possible if we never stop hoping."

Observing

Autumn 1990

"Grampa Joe, where does the light go when the dark comes?"

"It . . . goes . . . off?" Grandpa Joe answered more as if asking a question than stating a fact. "Why don't you ask questions that a normal seven year old asks? You're too smart. Did you know you can be too smart?" He slowly moved his eye from his telescope to his grandson.

"No, Grampa. Off isn't a place. I wanna know where the light goes when it leaves this room. Like, let's say I leave this room. I'm not here, so we both know I'm somewhere else. I'm roller-blading or reading, or I'm talking to Mom or going to the bathroom . . . you know? I don't just disappear. I go somewhere. So where does the light go?"

Joseph Keller and his grandson Paul Stone, each with his own telescope, sat together in the stargazing room of Peter and Rachel Stone's Lamplight Estates mansion. The stargazing room rested on the top of the second floor of the exquisite home. Rachel had imaginatively designed the room to look from the outside like a castle tower, and the room's express purpose was for watching the stars. Large clerestory windows extended around the circumference of the turret-like room, allowing both sunlight and starlight to visit on a regular basis. The octagonal shape of the room provided space for a number of telescopes, which graduated from rudimentary and old to the state-of-the-art Meade.

The room's soft silver carpet blended with the silvery wallpaper to create an atmosphere of peace and tranquility. Rachel liked to call this room her "celestial sphere." She escaped here to calm her fears and often to pray. She felt she could communicate more clearly with God in her stargazing room. This was the one place she could escape the sadness she'd felt since her mother's unexpected death six years earlier. The difficult circumstances that had surrounded the death made it even harder. More recently, Rachel was again spending increasingly more time in her "celestial sphere."

Forty-four-year-old Rachel Stone stood silently at the entrance to her stargazing room. Normally she would have used the intercom to call everyone to dinner, but she wanted to see for herself what these two were up to. She observed, hoping to be undetected, from the doorway, and she couldn't help but think how her seven-year-old son reminded her so much of her little brother, Joey, at that age. Their physical characteristics were uncannily similar—same blond, unruly hair, and identical soft blue eyes. Both lived for fun. As she listened to her son and her father, she thought about years earlier when her father used to talk like this with little Joey—Joseph Jr.

Joseph Sr. was an avid stargazer. The hobby fit his personality well. He was a man of few words who seldom, if ever, mentioned feelings or emotions, except when telling stories about the constellations. He could sit for hours in silence and search the sky. The longer he lived, however, and the better he got to know his grandchildren, the more his personality opened up. He was gradually becoming less guarded than he had been when Rachel was younger.

Rachel recalled the only time she remembered him saying, "I love you." It was when he had said good-bye to her mother just before the funeral director closed her casket. In fact, that was also the only time she had ever seen him kiss her mother. He had always seemed so strong—so in control—but at that moment, he had looked totally vulnerable and completely at God's mercy. She remembered thinking, "Now I know why Dad doesn't deal with emotions—he doesn't want to admit weakness."

Joseph's treasured stargazing tradition had passed itself down like a precious antique to his second daughter, Rachel, and to Rachel's youngest son, Paul. Though Paul was the only truly converted stargazer of the bunch, every grandchild in the family adored their tranquil grandfather. Though quiet most of the time, he was a tease, and he had learned to thoroughly enjoy spending time with the children. One night, a while ago, Rachel had come in and found them all, nine grandchildren and their grandpa, underneath her huge dining room table playing campout and listening to Grandpa Joe's hunting stories. Grandpa Joe really loved to hunt. He was a good hunter, and he liked to tell the kids about his hunting expeditions, and about the dark nights in the woods, where no city lights obscured his view of the stars. He had actually stuck glow-in-the-dark stars in the shape of several constellations on the underside of the table, and they all lay there in the dark looking at the stars and learning about the sky.

Rachel had seen a huge change in her father since her mother had died. He was more open. He had grown able and determined to accept his own mortality, and he was becoming more emotional and less guarded. "How can he be so darn stubborn on some issues and yet so sweet with his grandchildren?" Rachel wondered. Grandpa Joe, as the four Stone children lovingly dubbed their grandfather, was the only family member with enough patience to attempt to answer Paul's never-ending questions.

"Maybe," Joe suggested, resuming his stargazing, "the light is always there, but we can't see it until someone turns it on."

"You mean it like hides until we tell it to come out?"

"Maybe . . . yes, maybe it hides."

"Well, where does it hide? Not in the closet because we could see it under the door . . . not under the chair, not in your pocket." Paul quietly left his telescope and crept toward his grandfather's shirt pocket.

Grandpa Joe pretended not to see him. "And not in your ears!" He grabbed and tickled Paul, searching his ears. "Maybe we should ask where the darkness goes when there is light. Perhaps the light frightens the dark away until it goes to sleep and the darkness dares to creep back in." Grandpa Joe thought out loud, still tickling. "Maybe light just changes into dark and then back to light. You know, like a mutating microcosm in the universe."

"You're weird, Grampa," Paul said, frowning. Then his eyes lit up. "No, I know. I know what happens." He tumbled to the floor and filled his cheeks with air, pretending to have a mouthful of food. "The light *eats* the dark." The small boy grabbed his mouth, made loud chomping sounds, held still for a moment and then, dramatically choking, threw himself flat on the floor and finished his sentence. "Then it vomits it up when somebody hits the switch!"

Grandpa Joe teased in his best know-it-all scientist voice. "That's it, my boy. The darkness is swallowed into the belly of the light . . . That's what happens."

"And then . . ." Paul leaped onto his grandpa's lap, nearly scaring the old man to death. "The light . . . digests it." They both pulled a face.

"You know what that would make it?" Grandpa Joe chortled. They laughed hysterically, grabbing their noses at the same time and jumping up to dance around the mostly dark room.

"That is so gross, Grampa," Paul said with a grimace.

"That's worse than gross, my boy. It's grotesque," Grandpa sneered.

"Putrid," Paul countered.

"It's the granddaddy of all stink and waste," they exclaimed simultaneously, as they had on several occasions before.

Then Grandpa Joe's laughter ended abruptly. He eased himself back into his big chair, and he hugged Paul. Holding Paul's head to his heart, he kissed the top of his grandson's head and whispered, "Where does the love go, when the hate comes?"

"What did you say?" Paul whispered.

"I said I love you."

"I love you too, Grampa." Paul burrowed his small head farther into his grandfather's soft shoulder and thought about the darkness.

Behind the door, Rachel quickly wiped her eyes. She knew that the past six years had at once softened and hardened her father. She felt so torn. She wanted to take away his pain, but she knew she couldn't. She wanted to tell him what she knew about Joey. But she knew she couldn't. Besides, she could barely deal with her own pain.

"Grampa, can I tell you a secret?"

"I dunno, can you?"

"When I'm alone in the dark, I feel scared, but when I'm with you, even in the dark I don't feel scared at all."

"Can I tell you a secret, Paul? Sometimes I get scared too."

"You gotta be kiddin' me. I never knew old guys got scared."

"Yup, sometimes."

"What do you do when you get scared, Grampa?"

"Usually I think real hard and ask myself what I'm so scared of. Then I tell myself to fix whatever it is that's scaring me. After it's fixed, I have a good laugh about it all."

"So, like if you were scared of the dark, let's just say for a zample."

"An example?"

"Yeah, for a zample. You're sitting in your bed and the light's off and you can hear weird noises. Then you start thinking something—or somebody—is under your bed. Then you see a shadow that looks like a headless horseman sitting outside your window. Then you start sweating and you know you're gonna be the next victim . . . What do you do?"

"Well, *for example,* I say to myself, 'Okay, Joseph, whatever you do, don't lose your head.'" He grabbed his head and grinned. "I say, 'Self, if you sit here in the dark, you're gonna die. If you get up, you might have a chance. Take a chance, man—get up and turn on the light.' So I get up, turn the light on, search everywhere, and discover that I've imagined it all. Then I hop back in bed and have a good chuckle."

"Do you leave the light on?"

Rachel interrupted. "Excuse me, you two stargazers. Could you get your heads out of the sky long enough to come and eat Thanksgiving dinner?" She smiled at the two.

They straightened their telescopes, and Paul hurried to the stairs, but then he stopped.

Grandpa Joe walked right past Paul's questioning stare. "Now what kind of question is that?" he asked as he started down the stairs. "Do I leave the light on?"

"Well, do you?" Rachel teased.

"Of course I leave the light on—Do I have 'stupid' stamped on the top of my head?"

Paul grinned and inspected his grandfather's bald head for the word "stupid" as it bobbed slowly down the stairs. The young boy enjoyed spending time with his grandfather in the room he called the "star room." It was the perfect place for him to get all of his questions answered—quiet, peaceful, and happy. Grandpa Joe was always happier in the star room. Rachel followed them to the dining room.

Joseph Keller had never been an outgoing man with anyone other than his family. But for some reason, people were naturally drawn to him. In his earlier years he had been skilled in guarding his privacy, and when he stayed with his daughter's family, the star room was his fortress. His behavior since his wife died had become increasingly unpredictable. Everyone liked that he was opening up more, but as he opened up, he sometimes showed unexpected emotion.

Joseph followed his grandson into the massive dining room, where the rest of the family was being seated. The Thanksgiving feast spread before the family was incredible. Like their Swedish ancestors, the family enjoyed large gatherings, especially on holidays. The glow of the Stone home shone forth from a hundred white candles, all reflected again and again in the mirrors that lined the oak walls, on the silver and pewter dishes, and even in the darkening window panes of the dining room. Small teardrops of candlelight flickered on wicks' ends down the long length of the dining room table. The sun had set, and dark clouds loomed outside. A hum of anticipation spread throughout the enormous dining room.

Peter Stone began seating the excited guests. His wife, Rachel, watched quietly. Sixteen dinner guests in all. Peter stood at the head of the table. "Rachel, you're here next to me, right?" She nodded her head. "And Joseph, you get the other head of the table."

"Can I sit by Grampa?" Paul queried.

"All right, Paul. You're next to Grandpa. Kids, fill in around Grandpa. Angela and Wally, since you're the oldest—after Grandpa Joe, of course—" he teased, "you're by me." Angela was Rachel's older sister. "Besides, I could use a talk with a good shrink. And Christina, I'll let you and Carl decide how you want to arrange the twins. We put their booster seats next to each other, but you can rearrange things if you'd like."

When they were kids, Angela, Rachel, and Christina had fit the sibling molds—Angela had always been the boss and Christina the baby. But as they matured and turned to their own families, they left those roles and became equals and friends.

They had all been devastated at their mother's death. They had planned on having her around for many more years. But they had adjusted relatively well, except for Rachel. She was still struggling more than the rest of the family thought healthy.

At last everyone was comfortably seated. "This is a table set for royalty, Rachel," Carl, Christina's husband, announced.

"Thanks, Carl. The kids get the credit. They set the table and lit all the candles." The twins, Daniel and Derek, were behaving like any four-year-olds—struggling to blow out every candle.

"Really, Rachel, I've never seen such an elegant Thanksgiving setting," Angela said. "Thanks, sis. You do such a beautiful job." She raised her goblet. "I think we should drink a toast to Rachel, our most gracious hostess, and to Peter, our generous host."

They all raised their goblets filled with sparkling apple cider and chanted, "To Rachel. To Peter."

Quite unexpectedly, Joseph stood. Emotions that he had not learned to deal with rushed through him. Normally he would have suppressed his feelings, but he didn't this time. His gaze rested on the empty place setting beside Rachel. His lips tightened and then paled. The blood quickly rose behind his cheeks and reached the top of his mostly bald head. Desperately trying to control himself, he grasped the back of his oak chair, and his knuckles turned white. He spoke in a low whisper. "Rachel, why must you persist in this charade? Remove that plate . . . please . . . and take away the chair, too. We all know they won't be used." His eyes darted around the table as if soliciting a challenge and support at the same time. He stopped at his daughter's face. "Rachel, why do you insist on including this at every family function? I've put up with it for two years now. It's time to end it—time to forget. Please take it away . . . now." He stood menacingly, waiting for Rachel to object.

But she didn't. She silently obeyed her father's orders. She took the dishes to the kitchen, and Angela removed the chair. The family was still. Even Paul found himself questionless, and the other children were similarly hushed. It was Peter who finally dared speak.

"Well, I suppose we should begin with a blessing on the food," he said. He looked around the table, but not a single eye met his. Everyone stared at their plates. "Okay, since we're at my house, I guess I'll say . . ."

Wally glanced at Peter, then quickly nodded toward Joseph. Peter looked at him in disbelief and gave him his best you've-got-to-be-kidding look. But Wally just nodded, so Peter finished his sentence. ". . . I guess I'll say . . . Joseph, would you please offer the prayer?"

Rachel looked at her husband in disbelief, and Peter held his breath, fully expecting a refusal. Joseph Keller wasn't the praying kind. In fact, Peter tried to remember if in his eighteen years of marriage to Rachel he had ever heard Joseph pray. He decided he had not.

Each family member uncomfortably fidgeted but refused to look up. Silence surrounded them and seemed too long. Finally, to everyone's great surprise, Joseph's gruff voice spoke. "Father, we give thanks for this food and for the bounty of blessings we find ourselves among. Amen."

Some of the family's tension dissipated with the words of Joseph's prayer, but like his curt demands to remove the extra place setting and chair, most of the tension hovered about for the duration of their Thanksgiving meal.

Once the pumpkin pie had been devoured, Joseph retreated inside himself, thanked his daughter for the meal, cleared his plate, and then silently made his way back to the stairs.

Joseph ascended the steps to Rachel's star room. He had resolved to squelch his feelings again and return to the comfort of his stargazing. Although he wouldn't admit it, he liked coming here better than using his own equipment at home for the reason that Rachel's room stood above the surrounding forest and overlooked the nearby lake. Because of the backyard's descending elevation, Joseph was able to see for miles even with his naked eye. With the assistance of the Stone family's sophisticated telescope equipment, he could find just about anything in the heavens. So, every chance he had, Joseph would come here and search the heavens for familiar objects. He knew that his emotions would stay controlled in his methodical and careful viewing. In his searching, he had sometimes found new and different perspectives of stars and constellations. All of these were carefully notated in handwritten journals, complete with diagrams and carefully drawn pictures. Joseph took his stargazing seriously.

To Joseph, there were stories out there in the heavens; some told and retold, others waiting to be discovered and explained for the first time. On this particular evening Joseph elevated the heavy Meade telescope with its electronic finding mechanism. The sun had set, but it was neither day nor night. Joseph's grandfather had always called this time the time of lighting candles. It was during these hours that one could find the first stars and wish upon them. Joseph wanted to make a wish tonight.

As the sun sank deeply behind the mountains on the horizon, Joseph searched for the first star. Remarkably, he identified a new light shimmering and undulating with incredible intensity. In fact, the object appeared to be more significant, perhaps even a comet. Just on the rim of the horizon the light glowed against the darkness in the sky. Joseph quickly focused in on it with the locating device. It was motionless. To his astonishment, his discovery was not a real star at all. Rather, when magnified, he saw that his newly discovered star was really a creation of earthly origin. Yet somehow it was different, special. He felt that he could reach across the space of miles and touch the light emanating from this wonderful man-made creation. He had discovered a new star. He secretly named it Winter Star.

Rachel spoke softly as she and her two sisters cleaned the dishes. The women had scurried the men and children into the basement to try to recover some of the merriment that should accompany Thanksgiving.

The three sisters had grown even closer since their mother's death. Their mother had been the loving force in the family, and when she died, the girls had been terrified of facing life without her. Though not one of them ever said it aloud, they had each secretly believed that their mother's heart attack was the result of her pain . . . a broken heart.

"Why does Dad have so much anger?" Angela whispered in her analytical first-child way. "For the first years of our lives, he never showed emotion. Now he's all over the place. What's going on? And why can't I tell what he's thinking? Wally says it's because he misses Mom and has never dealt with her death properly. Wally says—"

"I don't know all the technical psychological terms," Rachel interrupted, "but I do know that he misses Mom. And he misses Joey, too. But is it really anger? It doesn't seem like anger to me."

"You didn't think that was anger?" Christina looked at Rachel with incredulity. "That looked like rage to me."

Angela tried to analyze. "Well, anger is a secondary emotion, you know. Wally says that you feel another emotion first, like fear or sadness, and then if you don't deal with it properly, it turns into anger."

Angela always tried to help the family deal with emotions. None of them was very good at it . . . except Christina. She knew how she felt, and she wasn't often afraid to speak her mind. She was the youngest of the girls and the least patient with her father's unexplained actions. "Dad's always been this way—even before Mom died," she said. "I don't think Dad can be pleased, yet we all just keep trying. You know what I think? I think we're making fools of ourselves falling all over him—Daddy, are you comfortable? Can I get you a drink, Dad? What can I do for you? How can I serve you? . . . You don't want that plate there, Daddy dear? Okay, I'll clear it. Never mind that it's Thanksgiving and you just ruined our dinner. He makes me crazy. And he's always watching the stars. What's that about? If he'd check in and join us on *this* planet, maybe he'd find out that he has some pretty decent daughters."

"Be careful, Chris." Angela motioned for her sister to calm down. "Mom always said that of all of us, you're the most like him."

"Oh, no I'm not! Rachel's the stargazer. How anyone can sit there for hours and stare at the sky is a total mystery to me. But, Rachel, I do have to say that I agree with him on one thing—it may be the only thing—but we've got to let go of—"

"Of what, our memories? Or should we just give up our hope?" Rachel turned her back, fumbling to find something in the sink to wash. She shut her eyes tightly so that tears couldn't escape. "Dad can make me stop setting the place, but he cannot force me to forget how I feel. I refuse to stop loving . . . and remembering . . . and hoping. Dad says he can forget, but look at him—he's not exactly the poster boy for happiness, is he? He hasn't stopped loving or remembering. He's only stopped hoping. Of all people, I thought you two agreed with me in what I've been trying to do."

"Rachel." Angela put her arms around her little sister. "We've got to get on with our lives. Christina and I have discussed this, and we're worried for you. It's like you're obsessed with it. You think about it constantly. You used to talk about it incessantly, and now you don't say a word, you just do bizarre things—like setting an extra place at the table. You and Peter are even fighting about it. Think about it—you and Peter have never disagreed on anything before, but this is really causing the two of you some problems."

Rachel started to explain why she had set the extra place again, but then she remembered her promise not to talk about it, so she changed her thoughts abruptly and asked, "How did you know that Peter and I are fighting?"

"Peter told us. He's worried about you, Rach. He talked to Wally and asked his advice on how to help you be happy again. He didn't share any of the details of why you two are fighting because he said you asked him not to talk about it. He just said that he can't seem to help you be happy again."

"Oh great! So my husband thinks I'm crazy. He's even consulted a shrink! That's just wonderful. You've all discussed this and decided what I should and shouldn't do. Are you planning to admit me to a mental hospital? Did anyone care to find out what *I* think?"

"This is even affecting your kids." Christina tried to smile. "And they've always been so secure. We think you need to let go of it. You need to realize that things change, but life goes on. We lose loved ones, but we have to carry on. We have no control over that."

Rachel refused to look at her sisters. Christina put her hands on Rachel's face and turned it to her. "You can't hold on forever—it's not healthy. We can't live on memories alone. Life's too short."

Christina rarely ever shed a tear, but even she dabbed at her eyes with the dishtowel. "I'm sorry if we hurt you, Rach, but you've got to know we're right."

Rachel swiped at her tears and calmly turned to face her sisters. "You *are* right. Life *is* too short." Rachel turned back to the sink and scrubbed at the gravy ladle.

Christina winked at Angela as if to say, "We're good. We've convinced her." But Angela responded with a that-was-too-easy look.

Suddenly, Rachel swirled around to face them again. Eyes wet, wild, and glistening, she pointed the gravy ladle in their direction. Soapsuds and water flew. Then squinting her eyes and pursing her lips, she calmly and softly whispered, "Thank you both for reminding me. Life *is* too short—*much* too short. It's too short to ever give up. I'm afraid I had started to waver, to give up hope and quit trying, but you two are absolutely and eternally correct. Life is too short. Thank you. I will *never* stop hoping."

* * *

Spring 1972

"*Come on, Rachel. I'm just having fun. Don't you remember what it feels like to be seventeen, sis?*"

"Joey, I'm hardly dead yet. Twenty-seven is not that old. I'm just concerned. I've been watching you, and lately you seem . . . I don't know . . . sort of mixed up."

"I'm not mixed up. I'm totally fine. In fact," he teased, "I'm so good, I feel like I could fly." He held his arms out and jokingly ran circles around his sister.

Rachel just shook her head. "How are your grades? Junior year is a biggie. If you want to get into college, you've got to at least go to class." Rachel tried to get serious. "Joey, I'm not stupid. I see what's going on. You're cutting class—a lot! You're fighting with Mom and Dad—you never used to do that—and you hardly ever visit with me anymore." Rachel pretended to pout. "We've always been so close, and I hardly see you now. I miss you. I miss our fun and our games. I miss seeing you happy."

"Look, sis, you worry too much. I'm telling you, I'm fine."

"Joey, you're not fine. I think you're in trouble. Don't lock me out. Let me help you . . . please."

Joey was aggravated. "Leave me alone. If I needed your help, I'd ask. If I needed anybody's help, I'd ask."

"But Joey, don't you remember how we used to watch the stars together? I miss those times. We used to have such good talks—about the girls you liked and all your friends. I don't even know these new guys you're hanging out with."

"Come on, Rachel. They're my friends. For the first time in my life I feel like I fit in. I feel like I'm a part of something. These guys accept me. They like me. They laugh at my jokes. They think I'm funny."

"But is that really what you want to be a part of?"

"Whatsa matter, Rachel? Don't they look good enough? Don't they fit into your rich-banker's-wife mold? Who are you to judge me or my friends? I don't need to hear this *from you, too. Mom and Dad are always hounding me. Why can't you all see that I'm just having some fun?" He winked at Rachel and turned to leave. "I'll only be seventeen once, you know."*

Rachel watched him walk away, and she thought how handsome he was. The shimmery blond hair and incredible muscles came from his participation on the high school swim team. But the magnetic smile was just from being Joey.

"Hey Joey," she called after him, "why did you quit the swim team?"

He answered without turning around. "Didn't quit. They suspended me."

"Why? You were in line for a state championship."

"My grades—anyway, I wasn't having fun anymore—too much work for too little pay." He stopped, then turned and grinned at her. "Besides, only geeks swim. And I've changed. I'm not a geek anymore."

As he drove away, Rachel observed, "You're right about one thing: You certainly have changed."

Laboring

Early December 1990

"Rachel." Peter spoke carefully. "It's nearly Christmas—only two weeks away. I've watched you go through all the motions. The trees are up and decorated. The presents are bought, wrapped, and under the tree. You've baked enough to feed the multitudes—sugar cookies, gingerbread, casseroles—all in the freezer waiting for the holidays. The house looks great inside and out!" Peter held Rachel by her small shoulders and turned her to face him. "But you're not really here."

"What do you mean, not here? Of course I'm here. You're the one who's not here. You spend as much time as you can at the bank so you don't have to 'deal' with me."

"Well, you gotta admit, 'dealing' with you has not been the most pleasant experience for the past while."

Rachel pulled away and faced her husband defiantly. "I have complied with all your wishes—" she turned away so he couldn't see her tears— "or should I say *demands,* haven't I?"

Peter looked puzzled. "What demands have I put upon you, Rachel? I haven't demanded that you do any of this Christmas stuff. I thought you liked decorating and baking and shopping and wrapping and—"

"I'm not talking about all of that." Rachel looked at him, this time pleadingly. "You're right, you don't demand any of this. It's not what you ask me to do that bothers me. It's what you expect me *not* to do that makes me crazy."

"Oh, so we're back to that, are we?" He hung his head and let out an exasperated sigh. "I can't talk about this right now. I've got to get to the bank. I've got so much to do. You know this is my busiest time—people need money, and they want their affairs taken care of before the year's end." Peter grabbed his coat from the hall closet and started toward the garage. Rachel hurried after him in her bare feet and robe. "That's right. When you don't want to discuss my family problems, you've just got too many important people to help. What about me, Peter? How important am I? I've tried to stay quiet about this because I know you don't want to discuss—"

"Don't want to discuss it?" he shot back. "That's all we talked about for the first year after your mom died. I'm talked out. It's been six years now, and—"

"And for the past two years, we haven't discussed it at all." Two years before, Rachel and Peter had agreed to disagree on the topic of her family because every time they tried to talk about it, they ended up fighting.

"That's right, we haven't. And it has been heaven."

"Maybe for you, but not for me. It's been hell for me. I feel like this is a huge part of me—who I am and what I am. And you have simply chosen not to be a part of it. I feel hurt. Everyday I feel so alone. You forbid me to talk about it, but I know you're aware that I've still been working on . . . things."

"Yes, I know you have. I see the signs everywhere— court papers, calls on caller ID. I know you're doing things."

"Well, aren't you even the least bit curious about what I'm doing?"

"Rachel, I know what you're doing, and I don't agree with it. You know that. I don't believe you're helping."

"But how can you disagree when you haven't been a part of it for at least two years? You don't really even know what's going on now. There was a time when I really needed you to help and to be there. But I've learned to do it on my own now. So I don't need your help. I would just like someone I could openly discuss all of this with. Someone who could give me unbiased feedback. I haven't spent a dime of your money—other than gas money to drive here and there. Remember, that's another demand you made. So I don't know what more you want me *not* to do."

Peter looked tired. Rachel felt sorry for him for a minute as she watched him walk toward his car.

When he reached the car door he turned and looked at her intently. "I want you to be happy. I want my wife back—the one who is excited about Christmas and who concentrates one hundred percent on our family and our children. I guess that's selfish, but that's what I want." He got in his car and backed slowly out of the garage.

"Well, I want my husband back," Rachel called after him, knowing he couldn't hear her. "I want the wonderful prince who rides in on his white stallion and rescues me from . . . from everything. The one who doesn't fight and tell me not to feel what I'm feeling when I try to tell him the deepest desires of my heart. The one who helps me through any problem I may face. I guess that's selfish, too."

The grandfather clock in the hall chimed six loud chimes. Time to get the kids up. Rachel picked up the phone and used the intercom to call her four children to morning prayer and breakfast. She tried to sound cheerful, but she knew she didn't. "We should have had family prayer before he left," she thought guiltily. "Too many days begin and end like this one."

Rachel knew she must seem obsessive to everyone around her. And setting a place at Thanksgiving again had been a big mistake, but she hadn't been able to help it. She had really thought this Thanksgiving was it. It could happen, couldn't it? But it wasn't to be this year . . . again, and she knew she looked foolish . . . again. Now everyone in the family thought she was crazy.

Oh well, she knew she couldn't worry about what everyone thought. She had to do what she believed was right, so she persisted even if it did seem crazy to everyone.

The kids—Lizzy, Paul, Sara, and David—shuffled into the kitchen one at a time from youngest to oldest and plopped down at the kitchen table. "Where's Daddy?" little Lizzy whined.

"Dad's never here for family prayer anymore," Paul complained.

Sara rolled her eyes. "He never used to miss."

"Isn't that why we get up so dang early? So Dad can be here?" David muttered in his almost teenage voice.

"All right, guys. You know Dad's working hard. How about we pray for him instead of complaining, okay? David, you're the man of the house when Dad's gone. Will you please pray for all of us to be a bit more understanding?"

Rachel could see that her family was not well. Used to be that the holidays brought out the best in everyone, but this year was bad. The Christmas spirit was not a part of the Stone home.

Christmas music could always bring good cheer. After the prayer was over, Rachel put a Christmas CD in the whole-house stereo system. But the Carpenters' serene suggestion, "Have yourself a merry little Christmas, let your heart be light. From now on your troubles will be out of sight . . ." seemed an impossibility for the struggling family.

Things went from bad to worse over the next thirteen days. The extra pressure to be jolly seemed a burden the family could not bear, and by the time Christmas Eve arrived, the tension was so bad that every little thing brought quarrels.

Grandpa Joe arrived around 9:00 A.M. For the past six years, at Rachel's insistence, he had spent Christmas Eve and Christmas Day with Rachel and her family.

Usually, Peter saw eye to eye with his father-in-law, but even their relationship had been strained by all that had happened since Mary's death. What had once been marvelous Christmas holidays had degenerated to actions without thought and tradition without meaning. No one seemed to feel anything good anymore.

When he rang the doorbell, Peter greeted him. "Joseph, thanks for coming. I know you really didn't want to, but I think Rachel and the kids need you. It seems like we just haven't been able to get the Christmas spirit. Rachel hasn't been herself the past while—ever since . . . um . . . and I haven't been real helpful to her, and the kids feel it too, and I feel horrible . . . But enough of that. Thanks for coming to spend Christmas with us."

The kids loved to have Grandpa Joe come. He liked to tease them and tell them that he had caught Santa in a trap and stolen all of his toys. The kids would argue back and forth about Santa's magic and his ability to escape any trap Grandpa Joe could possibly have set.

But even Grandpa Joe wasn't teasing today. He seemed too serious and the kids were disappointed that he didn't greet them with some outlandish story about having captured the jolly old elf at home in his stables. Little Lizzy even felt uncomfortable. "Hey, Grampa Joe—" she tugged at his coat sleeve as he carried his suitcase up to the guest room— "did you catch him?"

Grandpa Joe was distracted. "Did I catch who, Lizzy?"

"Santa, silly. Didn't you trap him again this year?"

"Oh, yes I did," he replied halfheartedly. "He's caught in my traps." He was terribly unconvincing.

"Where? How? When?" Paul started to question, but David stopped him.

"I think Grampa's tired, Paul. Why don't we let him rest before we interrogate him?"

David helped get Grandpa's suitcase into his room, and Sara hung up his coat. Then they closed his bedroom door and left him alone to rest.

"Wow, everybody's so Scroogey," Sara murmured.

"Yeah, even Grampa Joe's ornery," David agreed. "Christmas just isn't as fun as it used to be, is it Sara?" He hung his head and then slowly followed his sister down the stairs.

The Stone home was unusually calm for the day before Christmas. The kids were patiently waiting for their cousins to arrive. Maybe they could have some fun with them.

* * *

Summer 1980

The green Suburban turned slowly onto the quiet street. Rachel and Peter drove Rachel's parents home from Rachel's thirty-fourth birthday celebration. They were joined by Angela and Wally and Christina and Carl.

Rachel smiled at her family. "Thank you all for a perfect birthday dinner," she said. "It was so nice." Rachel hated growing older, but spending her birthday with family somehow made it bearable.

"Hold still, Rachel," Wally cautioned as he reached forward over the seat and yanked a hair from her head. "Look, it's a gray one."

The Suburban neared the cozy Keller home, which rested toward the end of a quiet country street.

"Oh, hush, you tease." Rachel turned around in her seat to give him a good-natured glare. "I already noticed just this morning that two extra wrinkles and three new bulges arrived— uninvited, I may say—on my birthday." Everyone laughed.

"Pull over, Peter!" Joseph warned. "There's an ambulance behind us."

Peter was already watching in his rearview mirror. "I see it," he replied, "but it doesn't have its lights or siren on. It's actually been following us since we turned onto your street."

Mary turned around to see. "That's odd. I hope there hasn't been an accident."

Peter pulled over, and the ambulance drove past them and moved stealthily down the street. Christina tried to calm her mother. "They do that sometimes, Mom. They take practice runs all around town so they will be able to find addresses in an emergency. I'm sure it's nothing."

Before Peter could pull back onto the road, two police cars, also without lights or sirens, sped past them. Then two more. And one more—a total of five.

"That is really weird," Rachel said with a scowl. "I've never seen so much excitement in this neighborhood."

Peter cautiously pulled back onto the road. "They certainly seem to be in a hurry to get somewhere, don't they?"

"Yes, they do," Rachel agreed. "Wait a minute . . . It almost looks like they're going to your place, Dad."

"Oh, mercy! They're stopping in front of our . . ." Mary began to cry. "Oh no, not Joey. What's wrong? Not Joey. Please don't let it be something bad!"

What happened next was like a scene from a horrible movie. Peter pulled over and stopped again, thinking that Mary and Joseph shouldn't have to see what he feared was happening at their home.

The ambulance and police cars stopped at the Keller home. The ambulance doors burst wide open, but instead of EMTs, an explosion of black ninja-looking creatures carrying huge guns emerged. They hit the ground and dispersed. At the same time the police cars spewed forth more of the same threatening creatures. In an instant, they surrounded the house. Four ninjas lined up on the front porch and used a post of some sort to ram the front door. Two hits of such force blew it wide open.

In the Suburban, everyone sat silently, not knowing what to say or do.

Finally Rachel said, "Shouldn't we go in?" She was crying now, too.

"I doubt they'll let us," Joseph responded quietly. His voice trembled when he spoke. "I was afraid of something like this. Joey's behavior has been so bad lately, and the crowd he's been running with are rough-lookin' characters."

Wally was putting everything together in his mind. "It's the drugs, isn't it, Joseph?"

"I'm afraid so." Joseph put his hands to his head. Mary continued to cry.

Christina was horrified. "The police are raiding the house, looking for Joey's drugs? Why do you let him live with you? We all know he's a mess. Do you let him bring drugs to your house?" She knew he had been heading for trouble, but she hadn't realized how bad it really was. She was so angry she couldn't sit still. She reached for the door. "I'm going over there. I'm not going to sit here and watch them destroy your house. Joey has hurt us all for the last time. What a waste— what a waste of a perfectly good life. He deserves exactly what he's getting!"

Rachel ignored her sister and reached back to try to comfort her mother. "Please try to relax, Mom. I'm sorry you have to see this."

Christina jumped out and Joseph followed her. They ran toward the house, but an officer jumped in front of them. They told him who they were and pushed their way forward. Two uniformed policemen shoved Joey and his two cohorts, handcuffed and face down onto the front lawn. They made them lie there like trapped animals. Then when the other officers were ready to leave, the policemen forced them to their feet and shoved them at gunpoint toward one of the waiting squad cars.

"Just a minute," Christina called. "I've got something to say to him." She pointed at Joey. The two policemen stopped but continued to hold Joey firmly by his arms. Father and sister stalked toward Joey, who hung his head in shame. Christina spoke clearly and deliberately.

"I hate you, Joey Keller! I hate everything you are. Look at you. You're pathetic! This is how you choose to repay Mom and Dad for all they do for you? I hate you."

Joseph stepped forward, and Joey looked up at his father, pleadingly. "Dad?" But what he met was an ice-cold glare.

"You aren't my son. My son would not behave like this. I refuse to watch you destroy yourself. Ever since you got mixed up with those so-called friends of yours, you are not the same. If you love your drugs more than your family, then go ahead and have them. Don't you call me Dad. I'm not your father. And you are not my son."

Joseph turned and walked away. Christina did the same.

The second ambulance that was summoned to the Keller home that night took Mary Keller's lifeless body. The paramedics tried to resuscitate her, but it was too late. Rachel told herself that God had simply stepped in and rescued her mother—let her die quietly of a heart attack in order to keep her from the torturing ugliness of Joey's drug addiction and all that accompanied it.

* * *

Christmas Eve 1990

The light of day faded into the same grayness of the clouds, leaving only a pale wisp of pink light to outline the mountains. December always brings the earliest sunsets. Without the sun, a hard unrelenting cold set in—the kind of cold that causes foot-stamping and nose-covering. Soon the cousins would arrive and the Stone children could begin their Christmas Eve merriment. As Rachel decorated her Christmas Eve table, she glanced out the window in the large dining room. The soft light of a street lamp was the only warmth in sight. Vaguely, she thought she saw a dark figure move along the lengthening shadows of the surrounding foliage outside in defiance of winter's cold. She stepped closer and touched the cold window.

Could it be? The wind appeared to push against the hooded figure, causing the heavy woolen fabric to billow among falling snowflakes. Without warning, swirls of powdery white twirled upward in front of cold gusts. The figure, seeming cautious not to be discovered, stood firm against the wind and the snow, shifting and leaning to capture a glance of the festivities inside the Stone mansion.

Rachel was filled with hope. She ran to the kitchen and, like she had done many times before, grabbed another place setting, made room for it on the table, and shoved in another chair. Then she hurried back to the window. This time she saw only her sisters and their families. They pulled up and bounced out of their cars. The figure had disappeared as cleverly as it had appeared. She rushed to the kitchen more excited than she could ever remember being on any Christmas Eve in her life.

The big clock chimed five lovely chimes. Dinner was ready, and *everyone* was here! Paul and Lizzy sat calmly on the entryway floor beside the three Christmas trees under the stairway, drawing pictures for Santa. The scent of pine filled the air with anticipation. The children hovered near the door, and Paul and Lizzy sat, waiting to see what would happen when everyone entered the house and stood below the mistletoe dangling from the entryway chandelier.

At last, the door opened and Christina and Angela and their happy families sang out, "Merry Christmas! We're here."

"Let's eat!" Wally called. "Something smells delicious, and we're starved."

Lizzy stood up, giggled, and pointed to the mistletoe. Wally followed her gaze. Then he grabbed Angela and swept her into his arms for an exaggeratedly long kiss.

"Finally! Somebody's here to have fun," Paul shouted and danced around the bright red poinsettias clustered near the big clock.

Carl winked at Christina as they all removed their snowy boots. Christina immediately picked up on his idea. Stocking footed, she and Carl chased Lizzy and Paul and the rest of the children down the wide hall. "We wish you a merry Christmas," they chanted through the kitchen.

Peter greeted them warmly, and Rachel laughed out loud as she hugged them and welcomed each one enthusiastically. Rachel so enjoyed having family gatherings. She had decided beforehand that she would make certain not to give anyone anything more to worry about. She had tried her best to be cheerful. She had been determined not to let anyone see that she and Peter were not getting along, and she had asked Peter not to tell anyone that she was a basket case. He objected, of course, and said that he had never said she was a basket case. Like everything else they tried to talk about these days, it had led to an argument. But, in an instant, the shadowy figure outside had changed everything. Rachel's heart swelled with hope.

Rachel was certain, now, that this Christmas Eve dinner would be a pleasant experience for everyone—and especially for Peter. She loved him so much, and she longed for the "good ole days" before everything went wrong. She felt so bad that they couldn't stop being mad at each other.

She wished many times that her mother were there to offer her some advice. She found herself thinking about her mother constantly. "How would Mom handle this? What would Mom do?"

"I'll be home for Christmas . . ." played softly on the whole-house stereo system.

In the kitchen, Christina hugged Rachel. "How are you doing, sis? Everything looks perfect, as always. But how are you doing . . . really?"

"I'm wonderful, Chris. Really I am."

Angela rounded the kitchen corner. "You look wonderful. And so does everything. Tonight's going to be the best. You look happier than I've seen you in a long, long time." She kissed her sister on the cheek and hugged her for a long while. Christina joined them.

Rachel was ecstatic. She always felt good when she had her sisters around her. She knew they loved her even when she was the most unlovable. They were always there for her. What peace! What comfort! She couldn't hold back her joy. Rachel knew she could trust her sisters, and she dismissed her resolve not to talk about the past. She was too excited not to share her news with them.

"I've got something to tell you two," she whispered, eyes sparkling with excitement. "But you've got to promise not to say a word." She paused, thinking maybe she shouldn't tell them yet. After all, she couldn't be certain. But then who else could it have been?

Peter interrupted the sisters. "Rachel, are we ready to eat?" Rachel threw her arms around him and, to his great surprise, kissed him right on the lips—something she never did in public.

"Okay. Let's dance, my love." She smiled brightly, looking into his eyes. "Do you know how very much I love you?" Peter was thoroughly surprised, but he was completely enjoying his wife's jovial state.

Angela watched in disbelief. "I think she's better."

"Amazingly so," Christina agreed.

"Let's dance," Peter smiled. The soft melody played, *"Please have snow and mistletoe and presents under the tree . . . "* Peter held his wife in his arms, looked into her sweet face, and waltzed her past Angela and Christina as if the two sisters were invisible.

As they passed, Rachel whispered her secret. "I set a place at the table for . . ." Her voice was muffled by the music. She and Peter danced like two young lovers reunited after a long separation. They waltzed their way into the dining room, and the rest of the guests followed almost reverently.

Paul saw his parents and immediately had questions—lots of questions. "Hey, what's going on here? Aren't Mom and Dad still fighting? They've been arguing all day. They're dancing. How come they're dancing? I haven't seen them dance for a long time. Have you seen them dance, David?"

David shrugged. "Be quiet, Paul. Don't ask so many questions."

"I'll be home for Christmas, if only in your dreams." The song ended.

"It's perfect, isn't it, Peter?" Rachel kept one arm around Peter and looked at the family surrounding her elegant Christmas Eve table.

* * *

Autumn 1980

Rachel walked timidly down the long corridor. Finally, she found him. Joey glanced at Rachel through the glass of the jail's visiting area. Then he lowered his head and eyes in embarrassment. She picked up the black phone and motioned for him to pick up on his side. He responded reluctantly.

"Why'd you come, Rachel? I'm responsible for my own actions—turned twenty-four last month, you know. Nobody has to take care of me anymore."

"*I know that, Joey. I came because I care about you. I know you're addicted and you need to get some help. The help I've been giving you—bailing you out of jail, giving you money, and all of that—has not helped you. I've actually enabled you to keep using. I thought I was helping, but now I know I wasn't.*"

Rachel felt like a broken record. She was always telling Joey he needed help these days. The fact is, the only times she saw him were when he was in jail or needed something from her. She ached for him. She wanted to help him so badly. But over the years she had learned very painfully that helping an addict who doesn't want to get well is impossible, no matter what you do.

"*Could you bail me out, sis?*" Joey had resorted to begging.

"*No. I'm sorry, Joey, but I can't do that this time. I love you too much for that.*"

"*What? If you love me, you'll get me out of this godfor-saken place.*"

"*Little brother, you're gonna have to get yourself out of the 'godforsaken place' you've dug yourself into. I love you. I'll help you get the right kind of help, but that's all I can do for you. So when you're ready to get help, you know where to find me. I'll be here. And I'll be hoping and praying for you. I know you can do it—if you want to. All I can do now is pray that you will want to . . . I mean really, really want to make the changes you need to make. You have options. You know what the judge said about getting some help in the drug court program.*"

Joey put his hand up to the glass, and Rachel touched it gently from her side. "*Rach, I don't think I belong here.*" He actually looked her in the eyes—a first in a very long time. He wasn't high—also a first in a long time.

43

"I don't think you belong here either, little brother."
He stood abruptly, but not before she saw the tears springing from his eyes. He shuffled to the door and left the visiting area.

* * *

Christmas Eve 1990

The family took their places at the festive Christmas table adorned with miniature Christmas trees with battery-operated lights. Beneath each tree lay an assortment of Christmas symbols: bright silver stars, shepherd's crooks, gold, frankincense, and myrrh. In the center of the table was an exquisite hand-carved nativity scene complete with sheep, donkey, and manger. Grandpa Joe sat first, and, as usual, the grandchildren clamored to sit beside him. He held one twin on each knee. Christina tried to coax the twins to sit by her and Carl, but they refused so she didn't insist.

Clanging his butter knife on his pewter goblet, Peter stood and toasted. He smiled at Rachel. "To the Christmas spirit—and the magical powers it possesses."

Rachel stood, kissed her husband, and raised her glass. "I'll drink to that."

Wally winked at Angela, who laughed out loud. Angela then looked around the table, silently counting place settings. Surely she hadn't heard Rachel say what she thought she had said.

Wally noted his wife's concern at once. "What's wrong?" he whispered. "You look sick."

"I am sick. Count the places."

Wally knew without counting. "She did it again. Rachel's got a problem, I'm afraid. When your dad notices, he's gonna blow . . ."

Angela watched her father during the prayer. He didn't close his eyes. Instead, his gaze moved methodically around the table—counting not just once, but two times to be sure. As soon as Carl said amen, Joe stood.

"I will not sit at this table."

The light left Rachel's eyes. The children were still.

Peter quickly scanned the table, then spoke softly. "Rachel! Not tonight! It's Christmas Eve, for heaven's sake. What's wrong with you?" He stood and followed Joe, who left the table without another word. Joe headed for the star room upstairs. Peter went to his office and closed the door. Rachel's tears overflowed and fell one at a time onto her red tablecloth. She looked pleadingly into the faces of what was left of her happy family. She thought how strange they all looked. Only seconds earlier they had all been so happy. "Look at you," she said without feeling. "You have all lost your hope. You don't believe that it could happen. You think it's too late, don't you?" Her normally sparkling green eyes were dull and lifeless. "I'm sorry that you don't believe anymore."

Wally walked over to Rachel to comfort her. He put his hands on her shoulders. "Rachel, dear Rachel." He knelt beside her and looked into her eyes. "You have to let her go. She is gone. Your mother is *never* coming back. I'm so sorry, but you have to accept that. You have to grieve. Go ahead and cry. Cry until you can't cry anymore." Wally was worried about Rachel. Her behavior was so erratic— even at her mother's funeral Wally had noticed that Rachel had not cried like he thought she should have. She hadn't gone through the grieving process in a normal way. And setting a place for one's dead mother for two years—that was abnormal. He had expressed his feelings many times to Angela, and Angela had asked him not to say anything more about it. But when Peter had finally come to him to ask him for advice on how to help Rachel be happy again, Wally knew he needed to try to help.

Wally could feel Rachel's shoulders convulsing. She had buried her face in her hands. He encouraged her to keep crying. Everyone else, children included, stared at her with concern.

Unexpectedly, Rachel raised her head and lowered her hands. The kids were delighted: the adults horrified. Rachel wasn't crying, she was laughing . . . hysterically. Tears rolled down her cheeks, but Rachel was definitely *not* crying. She laughed out loud.

Relieved, the children joined in her laughter. Rachel hurried to the kitchen and brought in the food, all the while wiping her eyes and . . . laughing. She served her exquisite meal.

Wally, Angela, Christina, and Carl ate uncomfortably. But Rachel and the children enjoyed a grand Christmas Eve meal. Rachel told them Christmas stories and seemed to completely ignore the unpleasantness that had just taken place. When everyone was finished, Rachel sent the children downstairs to play some board games. "We'll have dessert later when our meal has settled," Rachel promised. She began to clear the table. Still chuckling now and then, she hummed Christmas tunes. The others tried to help with the dishes, but she refused. "Please, just sit and visit. I'll be finished in a minute and then we can all talk." So they sat quietly, secretly thinking and plotting what they were going to say to her.

At last, the table was cleared and Rachel sat. "Well?" She smiled expectantly at each of them. She calmly waited for someone to speak. The others exchanged worried glances and stared back at Rachel, not knowing where to begin.

"Why don't you begin, Rachel." Wally was in clinical mode. "And explain your feelings about your mom."

"No, I think I'll start, if it's all the same to everyone else." Christina spoke through clenched teeth. "Let's stop tiptoeing around and say it like it is. Rachel, we just went through this at Thanksgiving—the place-setting garbage. You know it bothers everyone to see you thinking Mom's going to come back from the dead and suddenly appear at your table. That's sick. You're sick! Mom's gone. We all love her, but she's gone. And setting a place for her is crazy. We think you're off your rocker, lost your marbles, nutso. Do you understand?"

Rachel smiled pleasantly and nodded. "Yes. Finally, I do understand, Chris." She chuckled again and wiped her eyes with the edge of the tablecloth. Everyone watched in disbelief.

"Then what in heaven's name are you laughing at?" Angela blurted out. "You're scaring us, sis."

"I know, and I'm sorry. All this time I thought you knew what I've been doing. But how could you know? I haven't told anyone. He begged me not to say anything to anyone. It's no wonder you think I'm crazy. Peter has known bits and pieces, and we have fought about Joey, not about Mom. But I haven't really even explained it all to him because he didn't want to hear any more about it. And since everyone has been so uptight about everything, I haven't mentioned it to anyone." As she stood, she laughed again. She walked toward the window and with her face toward it, began her story.

"This place setting is not for Mom. I know Mom is not coming back." Relief filled the room and rested upon each puzzled brow. She faced them so she could watch their reaction to what she was about to tell them. "This place setting is now and has always been for Joey." Their concern returned. Peter, who had been standing at the door, was drawn into the dining room by his own curiosity. He sat down to listen, but said nothing.

"Oh, beautiful!" Christina spoke as if Rachel were not there. "Now we know she's not crazy—she's just stupid." She looked at the others. "Does she think Joey's just going to magically appear at this table and join us for dinner one of these days?"

"I don't know, Christina," Wally said. "Why don't we ask her?"

"Why don't you ask her, Mr. Psychoanalyst," Christina replied sarcastically. "I'm lost."

"I'll ask her." Angela was still as concerned as she had been before. "Rachel, what makes you feel that you need to set a place for Joey every time we eat? You didn't start that until he and Mom had been gone for several years. What is it that triggered this behavior?"

Rachel could see that everyone was disturbed. "Joey believes that he caused Mom's death. He has been living with tremendous pain and guilt all this time, but every day he makes some progress toward forgiving himself for what happened. He has come a long way from where he was six years ago. He has changed his life in so many ways. You wouldn't believe all that he has been through. But he has begged me not to tell all of you about his work to change himself. He wanted to be sure he could really do it first. I dropped little hints to you all the time, but I guess you didn't pick up on them. I just assumed you all sort of had figured it out, but now I know how crazy I have looked to all of you. I'm so sorry."

* * *

Spring 1981

"But how do I help myself? I don't know how. I've gone so far wrong that I don't know if I can come back." Joey Keller spoke out of despair. His counselor, Monica, a white-haired, tough-skinned woman, listened carefully and then threw his questions back at him.

"How will you help yourself, Joey? You're the only one who knows that. But more importantly, do you want to help yourself?"

"I think I do," Joey mumbled. He was extremely tearful and almost childlike. He had been clean nearly three weeks, and he always became humbled and scared at this stage. He was forced to face his problems and himself without the drugs. It was horrible for him.

"You think *you do?" Monica shook her head. "That's not good enough. You've gotta want it even more than you want that next hit. If you don't* know *you want to help yourself, then nothing's gonna change."*

"Okay, okay. I do. I do want to change. I want to change more than anything in the world. I hate what I've become." Joey wept. Monica handed him a tissue, and he blew his nose and wiped his eyes.

Joey met with Monica every day after group sessions as part of drug court. Once in a while Rachel would stop in and visit with him after his sessions. He was embarrassed, but she would say, though they both knew it wasn't true, that she was just passing through and thought she could stop and offer him a ride or a burger at the drive-through. Almost always, he took her up on the lunch offer. He looked like he had missed more than a few meals. They would talk and just be together.

Rachel always knew when he had relapsed—he wouldn't talk. She got really good at being able to tell just by his mannerisms when he was up, down, or in between.

"So, how's it going today, Joey?"

"I'm going to jail for three days."

"Dirty drug test, huh?"

"Yeah. I messed up. But I stopped before it went too far this time." Joey's shoulders slumped and his head fell.

"That's progress, Joey. You didn't used to be able to do that."

"Yeah. I guess."

"Joey, look at me." Joey looked at her between french fries.

"You are doing better. Look how far you've come. You're staying clean longer and using less and less. You are making progress."

"I guess so."

"Don't look back. And don't give up. So you made a mistake. Look ahead now. You can do it. I know you can."

"I hope you're right, Rachel. I guess that is progress. At least I can hope. A couple of months ago I didn't have any hope." He smiled a forced smile and thanked her for the food.

"Can I give you a lift home?"

"Actually, I was wondering if you could drop me at the jail? That's home for the next three days. I hate that place, but I gotta go, or they'll put out a warrant for my arrest."

"Three days is nothing, Joey. You're the toughest guy I know. You'll be fine. I have faith in you." Rachel tried to encourage him. They pulled up in front of the county jail.

Joey slowly climbed out of Rachel's Suburban. He moved somberly, not wanting to leave the safety that she always represented to him. He stood and faced her.

"Thanks, Rachel . . . for everything . . . I love you."

Rachel cried again as she watched her little brother put himself in jail.

* * *

Christmas Eve 1990

"How do you know all of this?" Christina questioned. "Where is he? We haven't had contact with him since Mom died."

"I don't know where he lives. He asked me not to try to find him or contact him, but he has stayed in touch with me occasionally. Do you remember the night he left? Dad told us that we were to consider him dead."

"Dad said lots of things he shouldn't have said that night," Angela remembered.

"Yes, he did . . ." Christina was remembering as well. "And so did . . . I. Over and over, I've wished I had never told Joey that I hated him. I love him. I always have. I was just so . . . angry. So many times I've wanted to take back those terrible words, or at least have the chance to tell him that I didn't mean it." Christina, who never cried, was crying. "So he's okay? He's alive, Rach?"

"Oh, yes, he's alive, and as I said, he's a new man."

"So he's better now?"

"No, Chris, once an addict—always an addict. He told me he learned this in rehab. You don't ever get cured. If you're lucky—or blessed, I should say—you learn to help yourself before it's too late. But once you have been

51

an addict, you have to always remember that you are only one drink or one hit away from a relapse. That's how you help yourself stay clean.

"Joey chose to travel down a road that not many people ever return from. His choices took him so far away from everyone who really cares about him that he really could not find his way back.

"After he left home, his drug abuse got really bad—fast. He was using all the time. He only came around me when he wanted help—legally or otherwise. I helped how I could. He scared Peter, who was trying to protect me and the kids from the evils associated with the drug-using culture, and Peter was angry that I spent so much time trying to help him. He forbid me to give him any money, so I helped by spending time with him whenever he would let me. I drove him to court, jail, and rehab, and I tried to be with him as much as possible. Turns out Peter was right—you don't help an addict by giving him anything, especially money. Peter and I fought a lot about it. I felt like we should be willing to give him everything we've got—after all, we have so much. But Pete held firm, and now I know he was right about that.

"I watched Joey go from bad to worse—in and out of jail. My heart ached for him. The first time I saw him hand-cuffed and shackled, wearing the orange jail suit, I sobbed. I watched him lose everything: jobs, money, friends, future, family, and self-respect. He traded all that was precious to momentarily feed his addiction. And the scariest part of it all is that he truly believed that he was a better person when he was using. He believed that he was physically stronger and more able. He believed that he could think more clearly. He believed that the drugs made him more likeable. When he was using, he felt invincible.

"He dropped fifty pounds that year. His body became weak and frail. He could no longer concentrate or carry on an intelligent conversation. I saw him in all phases—high, low, and in between. Every stage was ugly. But through all of it I held on to my hope that he would someday decide to make a change—to search for the path that would lead him back home. I knew that if I stopped hoping, I would stop believing. And if I stopped believing, I would stop trying. So I kept hoping. It's not easy to keep hoping when everyone else has stopped, when intellectually you know it's stupid and naïve. But when hope is all you've got, you can't let yourself stop. You keep hoping, and you pray . . . a lot. That's all you can do.

"One day while we were at court facing a second-degree felony charge for illegal drug possession, the public defender mentioned a program called drug court. Joey would plead guilty to the charges, but if he successfully completed drug court, the charges would be dropped. I felt like my prayers had been answered. This was a way that Joey could get help. He agreed and thus began his journey back home.

"It was the most difficult year he said he'd ever experienced. He had to attend rehab meetings five days a week for about five hours a day. He had random drug tests three times a week. He got extensive counseling—group and individual—and if a drug test came back positive, which it did a few times, he had to spend some time in jail.

"I saw a light slowly return to Joey's countenance. He cleaned himself up. He got physically healthy again.

"Each week, he would appear before the judge to report on how he had done. He learned to speak up for himself, and he learned to admit when he was wrong. The

judge was an incredible man with lovely, kind blue eyes—
Judge Christianson—firm, fair, and consistent. I'll never
forget him. Joey learned respect for the law, for the legal
system, and for himself. But he told me recently that the
only way he was able to stop using was when he actually
got on his knees and asked for help. The process was so
long and so painfully difficult.

"After a year, Joey graduated from drug court. I
watched as Judge Christianson congratulated him and
wished him well. Then they embraced, and Joey's tears
dropped onto the judge's black robe. 'You saved my life,'
Joey whispered. 'No, son. You saved your own life. I just
gave you a chance,' I heard Judge Christianson whisper
back. 'Good luck. You stay clean now.'"

Rachel finished her story and looked around the
table. Everyone was amazed at what she had told them.
"Just before you all got here, I could have sworn that Joey
was out there. I have invited him to everything we've
done as a family for the past two years thinking he was
finally ready to come back." She looked to the window.
"But I guess I was wrong . . . again."

* * *

Two days after Thanksgiving 1990

*"Joey? Is that you, Joey?" Rachel hadn't recognized the
number on caller I.D.*

*"Rachel, I'm so sorry I didn't make it for Thanksgiving. I
really was planning to come, but we had a huge Thanksgiving
celebration here and it lasted forever. I couldn't leave. Please
forgive me. Actually I did come earlier that night. I walked
around outside for quite awhile, but I just kept hearing*

Dad's and Christina's last words. I don't know if they're ready yet, Rach."

"It's okay, Joey. But will you please come for Christmas Eve? At least think about it."

"I don't know, Rachel. I'd really like to . . . but . . . well . . . I'll see. I love you, sis. Thanks again . . . for everything. It's not that I don't want to . . . it's just that . . . well . . . I guess I'm afraid of . . . Oh, okay! I'll be there if I can. Don't wait dinner, though."

Rachel was so excited to think that Joey might come. She couldn't wait. She tried to ignore her concerns that maybe the others weren't ready to see him. She hoped they would all be as thrilled as she was. How she wished she could share with them all she knew about Joey's progress. He had made incredible changes in his life! She wouldn't believe it herself if she hadn't been through it all with him. But she continued to keep Joey's confidence. She wanted him to be able to trust her.

* * *

Christmas Eve 1990

"Rachel, why haven't you told us about all of this?" Angela asked. "How did you do it all alone? I should have been here for you. I should have done something." Angela really meant that.

"Believe me, so many times I wanted so much to tell all of you, but Joey needed to trust me. I knew I could not share any of this with anyone until he was ready. So I just kept setting the extra place . . . and hoping."

Peter stood and hugged his wife. "So, you finally see it my way, do you?"

"Yes, Peter, I've known for a long time that you were right about the money and about the importance of not neglecting our family to help an addict who didn't want to get better. I understand that now, but it was so hard while I was in the middle of it. I can't explain the pain I experienced and the helplessness I felt as I watched Joey try to destroy himself. I kept telling God that I would do anything to help him save Joey, and then I tried and tried to save him. What I had to learn was that only Joey could save Joey. Even God can't save you if you refuse to be saved. But I still think you were wrong about leaving him all alone. I think I did the right thing sticking by him through it all. We have all changed . . . a lot. And I will never—"

Peter put his fingers to her mouth. "I know, I know." He hugged her tightly. "You'll never, ever stop hoping."

* * *

Rachel was right. The figure she had seen outside her window had been Joey. But when everyone drove up, his courage failed . . . again. He kept hearing Christina and Joseph's last words to him: "I hate you!" "You are not my son!" He just couldn't force himself to ruin their Christmas Eve celebration. It wasn't that he didn't want to be a part of them again. It was plain and simple fear that kept him away— fear of rejection, fear of hate, and fear of the unknown.

Loving

Christmas Eve Night 1990

At evening's end, true to her promise, Rachel served dessert to her family: rich, gooey brownies with hot fudge sauce and pink peppermint ice cream.

Angela's and Christina's children, who usually complained about having to leave, had their boots and coats on before the last dessert plate was cleared from the table. Santa would soon be visiting, and all were anxious to get home.

"Good night. Merry Christmas," Rachel called as everyone drove out of sight. She and Peter and their four children stood waving. Then suddenly David ran stocking-footed into the snow and began throwing snowballs. The other children followed suit.

"Hey, you crazy kids," Peter called, pretending to try to stop them as they rustled by. "Get in the house."

"You'll catch your death out here without your shoes," Rachel warned. "Hustle on inside now, guys." The children quickly obeyed, and Peter pretended to swat each little bottom on its way into the house.

"Dad, you won't forget to turn off the security system tonight, will you? Santa's coming, you know," Paul reminded Peter.

"That shouldn't affect Santa. He'll come down the chimney, right?" David smiled.

Paul considered David's comment. "Oh, yeah," he agreed.

Snowflakes were slowly falling, but increasing in size by the second.

"Isn't it lovely?" Rachel looked into Peter's eyes. She was referring at once to the sparkle in his eyes that she hadn't seen for so long and to the soft, gentle snowflakes drifting to the ground. Holding hands, they closed the door and led everyone into the living room.

"Is it time for the treasure hunt?" Paul asked. The Stone family's Christmas Eve tradition was to follow clues to a secret spot where they would discover new Christmas pajamas. Earlier Rachel had secretly hidden the fuzzy, red-flannel nightclothes behind the marble mantel in the living room. Clues were hidden all over the house.

Sara was reading the first clue aloud to the family when they heard it: banging on the front door so loud that one of the paintings in the living room fell off the wall and crashed to the floor. Bells rang out, and a huge deep voice shouted, "Merry Christmas! Ho Ho Ho!" And the security system began to screech throughout the house and neighborhood.

Wide-eyed and completely afraid, Paul and Lizzy made a mad dash for the stairs. Paul yelled at the top of his lungs. "It's him! It's Santa. Get to bed everybody—hurry up! All of the children bounded up the cherry-wood stairs, not daring to peek at the front door. The loud voice thundered again from outside. "Merry Christmas to all!"

Paul could be seen from the entryway, scurrying nervously back and forth on the second-story balcony. "Turn off the alarm, Dad—hurry! It's him. It's Santa Claus! If you don't turn off the alarm, the police will come and arrest him, and we're not going to get anything . . ." It was difficult to discern which was loudest—Santa, the alarm, or Paul.

The house was in a complete uproar. David rushed to shut off the alarm while Peter and Rachel greeted the most authentic Santa Claus they had ever met. He appeared to be around sixty years old, maybe a little older, with stunning light blue eyes. Even Grandpa Joe descended to see the magnificent Santa. From the heavy black leather boots to the hooded cloak trimmed with white fur, the suit he wore was of an indescribable red-tanned leather. Its brightness was dimmed only by age and what appeared to be fireplace soot. The family stood still as if transfixed by his splendor. Then little by little each child inched down the stairs.

Under the cloak, Santa wore a set of loose-fitting leggings and an ample coat with splendid gold buttons. Each gold-lined button was a carefully crafted, colorful emblem. Next to his collar was a bright green holly-leaf button. Below the holly leaf were brilliant gold and silver star buttons. Nearer the coat's waist was a large green Christmas-tree button decorated with a red-and-white candy cane in the shape of a shepherd's crook. The final fastening piece, cleverly placed at a child's eye-level, was a manger filled with straw, cradling a baby nestled deep and wrapped in swaddling clothes. The buttons shimmered in the entryway light.

The children moved silently closer to enjoy the unexpected visitor. Lizzy noticed that the top of Santa's wooden staff was a carved face that perfectly resembled the man, and

Paul immediately noted that the neatly trimmed, white beard and bushy eyebrows were perfectly real—not the weird kind you see on a mall Santa. They inspected him completely, sneaking even closer. An old-fashioned, never-used, hardwood pipe dangled from a silver chain about his neck, and a pair of antique spectacles hung from the same chain. The pipe and glasses were suspended just above a thick, black belt adorned with an elegant holly-leaf clasp and silver bells—bells that made a distinct, familiar sort of sound.

"Hello, Peter," Santa said in a very careful, but heavy Scandinavian accent. "I am here on extremely urchent business. I tink you may be able to help."

"Well, uh . . . sir, I believe you might have the wrong address. You see, this is the Stone residence, and I think you may have mistaken—"

"Peter . . ." Rachel swung the door wide open, and invited the man in. "I believe Santa Claus has come to the right house." She stared curiously at his uncommonly handsome face. His transparent blue eyes were strangely familiar to her. She searched her memories and was puzzled. She knew he looked familiar, but she could not remember where she had seen him.

"Santa, Santa, I knew you would come. My Grandpa Joe set a trap for you and your reindeer, but I told him he'd never catch you. Then my Dad set that stupid alarm, and I thought maybe you wouldn't come because of the sirens, and . . . but I just knew you'd come!"

Lizzy kicked Paul squarely on the knee, and he shut up. Peter studied the old man carefully, thinking that Rachel had orchestrated the wonderful surprise.

"You see, Grandpa Joe, you didn't catch him after all. He got right past those darn nets you set for him." Lizzy

60

stepped forward with a crayon drawing of Santa's sleigh and eight reindeer, complete with a carefully drafted note, warning "WOCH OWT FOR MY GUMP'S TRAP." Paul produced similar notes and pictures for Santa, who knelt next to the children, collecting the notes and thanking them for their warning. Then Santa turned to Grandpa Joe.

"Vhat is dis . . . uh . . . you haf bin up to again, my dear friend, Joseph? You know dat . . . uh . . . you cannot catch my tiny reindeers. For years and years you haf tried vitout success. I tink dat you and I should make a truce. Vhat do you say?"

Grandpa Joe looked puzzled but then joined the fun. "Well, I think I may have already caught some of those reindeer of yours this year over at my stable, and I was hoping to sell them at a profit."

"Shame on you, Joseph. You know dat my reindeers are magic and can escape any trap you set for dem."

"Ah, but this year, I have come up with something stronger than those other traps I have used before."

"Joseph, you are very smart man. I tell you vhat. Eef you acree not to set de traps tonight, I vill geef your grandchildren a special gift to remember dis night—iss it a deal?" Santa extended his gloved right hand. Grandpa Joe hesitated just long enough to make his grandchildren squirm and then extended his own right hand. The children roared their approval.

Santa knelt again and drew a red satin bag from his waist. He reached deep inside and extracted a beautifully carved wooden tree ornament that happened to match the visage carved on his staff—the image of Santa himself.

"Dees iss for you, Dafid. I am liking dat you are de eldest child in dis good family. I tink dat twelf-year-olds sometimes lose da part off deir brain vhich help dem to imachin. I hope you do not lose part of your brain dis year. Each Christmas, as you decorate your tree, remember dis night and da true meaning of Christmas giffing. Now your imachination can help you to create vays to giff, radder dan receive."

David grasped the wooden ornament and Santa's message. He smiled knowingly at Santa and nodded. "Thank you, Santa. I'll do my best."

Next, Santa produced a handcrafted toy elf. "Dis iss for you, Sara, because you, like my elves, haf shown yourself for all off your ten years off life to be a true helper off mine. Treasure dis elf and remember dat it teaches you to be Christmas helper alvays." Sara thanked Santa and held the elf as carefully as she would hold a porcelain doll.

"And for you, liddle Lizzy, Mrs. Claus made for you your very own Christmas pillowcase. May you sleep vell and dream dat efry day iss Christmas."

Lizzy hugged the red-and-green polka-dotted pillowcase to her cheek and examined the two small brass bells fastened to it. She inhaled deeply. "Thank you, Santa. It smells so nice—like my mama's perfume."

Finally, Santa reached into his bag one more time and extracted a Christmas winter scene, the kind that comes in a glass bubble that snows when it's overturned. Inside the bubble, Santa and his reindeer were landing on a housetop. Paul immediately grabbed it and began to wind the key. The tune, "Here Comes Santa Claus," began to play.

"Is this really mine, Santa?"

"Yes, Paul, id iss yours to keep. Remember dis night and dat Christmas vill alvays bring da spirit dat you now feel. Da only trap dat can stop it iss your own unvilling-ness to spend da time and enerchy to vind it."

"I won't forget, Santa. I promise."

Peter Stone watched the Christmas magic that filled his home. "But, Santa, you said you needed our help tonight. What can we do for you?"

"Ah, Peter, tank you for reminding me. A terrible ting has happen. For some reason dis year my elfs haf forgotten to prepare Christmas for a family dat recently moved. It has been hard for my elfs to keep track of dis family and so ve forget to make deir gifts. I am trying to find da four children in dis family so dat I may fisit dem and beg deir forgifness, and so dat I might promise to fisit dem wid presents next year." Santa sighed heavily and opened his large, red Christmas list. He stared somberly at the names.

Peter edged closer to Santa and looked at the list. "What are their names, Santa?"

"Dees are deir names." Santa showed Peter his list. "De fahder of dis poor family recently suffered some misfortune, and I fear dat without me dey vill not vind Christmas dis year, and dere vill be a twelf-year-old boy, a ten-year-old girl, a sefen-year-old boy, and a four-year-old girl who vill not understan vhy Santa did not fisit dem."

Rachel stepped forward. "But, Santa, how can we help you?"

"I understand dat your husban iss very smart man and knows how to help people in need. Perhaps he can help me locate dis family."

"It's true, Santa. Daddy helps people when they need things—don't you, Daddy? He even owns his own bank and gives people loans and stuff like that," Lizzy explained.

"Yes. This is true, sweetheart. Let's see what we can find." Rachel was already thumbing through the telephone book, looking for an address.

"You won't find it there, Rach. I know where to find them. Part of their family farm was taken by the state in the airport expansion project. They wouldn't sell out, and in the end their land was taken by the government through eminent domain. Our bank handled the financing for the airport. The family ended up having to move into a trailer park near the lake," Peter said.

"Vhere iss dis place?" asked Santa.

"It's actually not far from here, except you'll have to dri—I mean fly over the lake to get there. Let me draw you a map."

Peter quickly drew a map with detailed landmarks while the children crowded in on Santa.

"Are you the real Santa?" asked Lizzy.

"Of course he is. Look at that beard," Paul said as he elbowed Lizzy in the side.

"Well, if he's the real Santa, then where are his reindeer, and why did he walk in our front door instead of coming down our chimney?"

Paul pondered these questions and simply turned to Santa, fully expecting an appropriate explanation. Peter handed Santa the map, which Santa carefully stuffed into his red woolen glove.

"Vell, as matter of fact, I did bring a couple off my reindeers on dis quick trip. Of course, de udders are resting up for da long chourney later tonight."

"Where are they? Can we see them?" the children yelled at once. Even twelve-year-old David was interested to see.

"I think you might be able to catch chust a climpse of dem. I gafe dem some carrots to eat and let dem go into da backyard." Santa walked confidently through the house to the ornate French doors that led to the deck that wrapped its way around the back of the Stone home. The children scurried behind him, trying to get to the deck first.

"Voa! Don't run up on dees two. Dey're liable to bolt avay, and I vill nefer be able to gadder Christmas. Stay right here, and I vill call dem so you can see."

Santa knelt down next to the back door and raised his index finger to his lips. Then he removed the glove with the map, revealing a leather wristband decorated with sleigh bells. He opened the door only slightly and gently shook the bells, making a faint tinkling sound. Magically, two sets of antlers appeared right next to the deck. The children squealed with joy.

"There they are!" Paul called to Grandpa Joe.

"Good heavens, I believe you're right," the old man chuckled.

"Now I mus be going or I vill be late for Christmas. Be careful not to scare avay my reindeers," Santa cautioned and then exclaimed, "Merry Christmas to all, and to all a good night!" Santa gathered his staff, his satin bag, and his red Christmas list and left through the front door. The children followed and then ran back toward the deck. David blocked the doorway as long as he could to keep the children from scaring the reindeer.

When the children finally got outside, they inspected chewed-up carrots and what looked like tracks made by sleigh runners. Peter looked both ways—up and down the street. He thought he saw a red Blazer without its lights waiting a ways away on Lamplight Lane. He was certain he had never seen the man dressed as Santa before. So how did Santa know him? How did Santa know he worked at the bank and would know this family?

The Stone family gathered on the deck with Rachel and Peter raising their eyebrows at one another. Rachel was certain she had seen this Santa before. But she still could not remember where.

"Look, everybody! Santa lost his glove and the map. Hurry, we've got to find him and tell him how to find the children's house!" Paul exploded through the front door of the house with the glove and map in his hand.

"He's gone. It's too late!" cried Lizzy. "Mommy, what are we going to do? The children won't have any Christmas."

Paul's shoulders slumped as he walked back to join his family with the map in one hand and the glove in the other.

Suddenly, David and his imagination burst into action. "I know! I know what we can do!" David grabbed the glove, ran to the family room, and dived under the giant Christmas tree. "Here they are. We'll help Santa gather Christmas this year." David stood holding three gifts with his own name on them. Sara and Paul followed David's example. Under the tree they scurried and began their own gathering.

"What are you doing?" Lizzy questioned, afraid she was being left out.

"Come here and we'll teach you, Lizzy!" Sara and Paul rejoiced as they explained their plan to their little sister.

"Children, are you sure you want to give away your own presents?" asked Grandpa Joe. But when he saw Rachel and Peter join the children in the gathering, he too was inspired to find something to share with those in need.

Thinking of the effort that had gone into Santa's Christmas Eve escapade, Grandpa Joe scratched his bald head and laughed heartily. It was apparent by the astonishment on Peter and Rachel's faces that neither of them was responsible for the memorable event. And the reindeer— what magical apparitions they were!

"Who was that, Peter? Did you set this up?" Rachel whispered so the kids wouldn't hear her. When Peter just shook his head, her forehead wrinkled in confusion. "He looked so familiar to me. I know that I know him. Oh, how do I know him? Where have I seen him before?" Rachel turned to Joseph. "Did he look like someone you know, Dad?"

Joe glanced at Lizzy's face and laughed out loud. Lizzy, hands on hips, was scowling at her mother.

"Of course he looked familiar, silly goose. He's Santa Claus!"

David quickly seized the chance to tease his mother. "Yeah, Mom! I mean, come on—red Santa suit, black boots, bells, white beard, Christmas Eve? Hello."

Peter joined the fun. "Yeah, Mom, and how about those reindeer? They should have been a dead giveaway. You know, St. Nicholas? Kris Kringle? Santa Claus? You remember him, don't you?" Then he whispered without moving his lips, "No, I didn't set this up. I thought you did."

Grandpa Joe looked nonchalantly at his daughter. "Yep," he said, winking at David, "Santa pretty much always comes on Christmas Eve, Rachel. You oughtta know that by now."

Joe was thoroughly and emotionally engrossed in the Christmas spirit that Santa had left, and quite unexpectedly he burst into a vigorous vocal rendition. "Joy to the world, the Lord is come," he belted.

Peter could not believe his ears, and Rachel looked at her father with astonishment. The rest of the family joined in his song as they gathered around the gigantic living room Christmas tree. Rachel led the singing with Santa's forgotten red glove on one hand, and she rested her other hand on her father's broad shoulder. ". . . let earth receive her King. Let every heart prepare him room . . ."

At the end of the carol, the excited family hurried for their coats, hats, mittens, and boots. They were all eager to be off in a flash to deliver the Christmas they had gathered for the family that wasn't going to get Christmas this year.

Just before they all piled into their black Suburban, Grandpa Joe turned and hurried back to his room. He returned a moment later with his binoculars hanging around his neck. He never left home without them. "Don't want to miss anything interesting," he always said.

Snowflakes blanketed the Suburban's windshield between each noisy swipe of the wipers, and the Stone family continued to sing their favorite carols. The roads were treacherously slick. Thank heaven for four-wheel drive and Peter's safe driving. Peter knew exactly where to go. He had actually seen the airport expansion's map, and on it was a small drawing of the streets, which led to the nearby trailer park where the forgotten family had been forced to move.

"How sad," Lizzy leaned forward and whispered to Grandpa Joe from the Suburban's very back seat. She and Paul always sat in the very back since everyone hated to lift the seat forward and it was easiest for them to climb over the seat.

"What's sad, my girl?"

"That Santa's family had to leave their home. And that Santa's elves forgot about them. And that they won't have much of a Christmas."

"Yeah, do you think they'll like the stuff we're bringing them?" Paul asked upon hearing Lizzy's whispers.

Rachel overheard the conversation, too. "I'm sure they'll love these gifts. You chose wisely." Paul softly shook the two packages he held and for the first time, he wondered what great gifts he was giving up. Lizzy and Sara and David did the same.

Rachel quickly diverted their attention, pointing across the way. "Look at that . . . light in the distance. Do you see it? I've never noticed that before. It's so bright. What is that, Dad?"

"It looks like a Winter Star to me."

"That looks very near where we are going." Peter studied the darkness. "It does look like a—star."

Grandpa Joe peered through his trusty binoculars. It was the same apparition he had first seen a few weeks ago on Thanksgiving night. "It is exactly that—a star. Imagine that! A new star in the heaven . . . Hmm . . . on Christmas Eve." Grandpa Joe studied the star. He could see that it seemed to grow out of the snowy hillside. The closer they got, the more beautiful the star appeared. Icy snowflakes made it magical, and all eyes searched the growing starlight as they traveled ever nearer to it.

At once the road veered sharply to the right, and they were no longer headed toward the star. "Hey, Dad, aren't we going the wrong way? The star is the other direction. Do you know where we're going?" Paul was concerned. He wanted to follow the star.

"I have to stay on the road, Paul. We're getting near the lake, and if I leave the main road, all that's out there are little unpaved roads—dangerously slick and muddy little roads in this stormy mess.

"Isn't that why you've got a Suburban?" Grandpa whispered to David, who sat beside him.

"Um, Dad, isn't that why we've got a Suburban? And four-wheel drive? And mud flaps . . . and . . ."

"No." Rachel squirmed. "That's not why we have a Suburban."

"Rachel, I'm afraid I have to side with David on this one. Yes, this is exactly why we drive a Suburban. Yee haw!" Peter pressed the gas and swerved wildly off the paved road. "Here we go." The Suburban bumped and lurched over the snow-covered, muddy field as the travelers moved toward the mysteriously beautiful star.

All at once, the snowflakes stopped falling and magically, the sky cleared directly above the family. Simultaneously, the strange star they were following hid itself as quickly as it had appeared, becoming invisible, as if it had never been there. Joe searched for it but was unable to find it even with his high-powered binoculars. A whirlwind of snow eerily encircled them, breathed heavily, and then fell dead to the muddy ground.

Peter was puzzled. "Well, I have to admit that I'm not quite sure where we are," he said. He knew this area well, but nothing was familiar now. He slowed and then stopped the Suburban. The compass on the rearview mirror had dimmed and become unreadable. Peter turned on the dome light to look closer at it, but it was of no use. They sat in silence. No one knew what to say.

Lizzy finally spoke, "But it's Christmas Eve, Daddy, and I want to go home." All around they could see no light. Only the whiteness of the snow-covered ground offered relief from the surrounding blackness.

* * *

Summer 1981

"*What made me go so far wrong? I truly don't know. I guess I never felt like I fit in, and I just never found my niche. I always felt, well, different. It's hard to explain. I felt like something was wrong all the time—like something was missing—but I could never fill the void. I tried to fill it with alcohol and drugs, but even that didn't get rid of the emptiness.*

"*I lived only for fun and excitement. I liked school and swim team, and even seminary, but then I started smoking a little dope now and then just for the excitement and to fit in with the guys I thought were cool. At first it was just occasionally, but then I thought it would be funny to go to those anti-drug assemblies at school stoned. So I did. I thought it was funny. I learned to lie with the best of them. I had a lie for everything. Marijuana is how it started. I smoked it to fit in at first. Then I liked that I didn't have to think—I could zone-out everyone and everything . . . completely. Mom and Dad knew something was wrong, but they had no idea I was smoking dope, sometimes right under their noses. That was okay for a while, but then I craved more. I wanted to feel good all the time.*

"*High school ended, and all my drug-buddies floated in different directions: prison, rehab, one even ODed and died. I no longer fit in anywhere. All the good kids were doing good things—school, missions, marriage. But not me. It's pretty ironic that the drugs I'd taken to fit in had turned me into a total outcast.*

"*The marijuana turned to smoking meth, and then to shooting it. The drug-induced euphorias grew steadily weaker, but my cravings only grew stronger. I wanted it all the time. It made me feel like a king—stronger, smarter, faster, better. I didn't have to sleep. I could go two or three days without rest—accomplishing more, so I thought. In reality, I was accomplishing nothing. Tweaking my life away into nothingness.*

"I lived for my next hit. I only feared two things—jail and death: Jail because I might not be able to use, and death because deep down, somewhere in my distorted little mind, I knew I didn't want to face my Maker.

"I did it all—horrible, unspeakable things. Even my thoughts were filled with filth. Always, after my two- to three-day, non-stop, meth binges, I had to crash. I woke up from those crashes in places I didn't even recognize—streets, gutters, parks, drug houses . . . jail.

"The fun was gone. I was completely addicted. I was used to quitting anything that wasn't fun, but I couldn't quit this. I tried—every couple of days—until I got low. Then I crawled, begged, and stole my way to my next hit. I was sick constantly. I had no immune system. My body ached everywhere. I'd always prided myself on my physical strength, but my body actually cannibalized its own muscles, and I became so weak that I couldn't get out of bed sometimes. Literally and physically, I surrounded myself with filth.

"My life was a total waste. The weekend parties melted into whole-week binges. I lost track of time, and before I knew it, I had lost two years of my life.

"I can only describe myself as totally hopeless. Even when I wanted to, I couldn't change. It got to the point where everyone—myself included—thought I'd be better off dead. I wanted to die, but I was too afraid of what would come after death. I tried to sleep as much as possible—to get as close to death as I could without having to account for my life.

Somewhere in the cobwebs of my mind I thought I remembered being told that if I didn't control my bad habits in life, I'd still have the same desperate, insatiable cravings in the next life. I couldn't bear that thought. I was trapped in a state somewhere between life and death, all the while heaping more condemnation upon my soul.

"The drugs stole away my ability to choose. It was hopeless to try to quit—I just couldn't. Mom and Dad tried to help, but they didn't know how. I was killing them, and I was dying a slow death myself.

"The night of the raid on Mom and Dad's house, I sank to an all-time low. My addiction brought death and destruction to the only people I really loved. Chris and Dad hated me, and I didn't blame them. I knew I had betrayed all of you.

"Rachel, I don't know why you have stayed around. I don't think I would have if I had been you. You believed in me when there was nothing to believe in."

"It's true, Joey. There were times when I wanted to give up—when I saw you torturing yourself like that. But I always believed that you could overcome if you would just fight. And when I prayed for you, the Lord told me you could do it . . . if you really wanted to.

"Finally, you were ready. I had learned that I could want it for you more than anything, but that until you wanted it, nothing would change."

"I'm sure grateful for you, Rachel."

"How are you, today, Joey?"

"I'm fine, today. But I have to take it one day at a time. I've been clean four months, two weeks, and five days, thanks to you, God, and drug court. They keep pretty tight reins on us in this program. But I've lost so much of my life. They tell us not to look back—just to keep looking to our future, but *it's really hard not to think of everything I've given up . . . all that I've lost."*

"Why don't you come to my house for the Fourth of July family picnic? It's going to be in my backyard—just Wally and Angela, Christina and Carl, Peter and I, Dad, of course, and the kids. We'd really like you to come."

"You *might* want me, but I guarantee the rest of them don't."

"At least give me your phone number so I can reach you. Where are you staying?"

"Out of jail—that's sayin' a lot for me."

* * *

Christmas Eve Night 1990

"Why is it suddenly so dark?" Paul cried. "Where did the light go?"

Grandpa responded quickly. "Okay, Rachel, what do we know about the stars?"

"We know it's winter, Dad. So we know that the winter stars are out."

"Good, and what else do we know, Paul?" Joe was now in his element and completely thrilled.

"We know that there is only one star that doesn't appear to move when the seasons change and the earth turns."

"Excellent, my boy."

"Polaris," Rachel added, smiling. She jumped out to search the sky. Joe followed, glued to his binoculars. One by one, the family filed out of the warm Suburban and into the cold, crisp air. All faces turned upward, hoping to find the star.

"I see it," Rachel called out, pleased with herself.

"Me too." Paul excitedly pointed out the North Star to everyone else.

David was impressed with their quick skill. "That's cool," he said.

"Now what, Grandpa?" Sara asked.

"Now we face Polaris." They all turned toward the star. "West will always be to your left, east to your right, and south at your back—always! Peter, do you remember in which direction we were headed when we saw the new star we were following?"

"Yes, now that you mention it. The compass on my mirror said we were headed directly east at that time."

"Well, now, aren't we wise? We just head east and follow our star. It will lead us to Santa's forgotten family." Joe loved to teach about the stars, and he especially enjoyed having a captive audience such as this. He remembered with fondness the time he and Joey had been seriously lost while hunting. He had taught Joey to be patient, to wait for Polaris, and then to follow Polaris to safety. How he missed Joey and wished they could still share their love for the stars. But that was a whole world away. Six years and too much hurt and ugliness had passed since then. Joe knew he had learned to be a better person since Joey had left. He was beginning to realize that he was more capable of loving his son now than he had ever been before.

Once they had all located the North Star and decided to use it to travel east, everyone seemed relieved. They climbed back into the Suburban.

"Dad," Rachel called to Joe, who stood oblivious to his family, watching the stars. He was remembering his lost son and the love they once shared. He was wondering how so much hate had slithered into their relationship. He thought how clever it was that Christmas had sent them on this star-following adventure. And how interesting that their journey was magically leading him to feel something for his son that he should never have stopped feeling. *Why now?* he wondered. *Where does the hate go, when the love comes?*

"Dad," Rachel called, interrupting his thoughts. "Are you going to stand there all night? We've got work to do, you know."

"Oh, right you are. I'm sorry. I was just . . . remembering." He turned and pulled himself into the Suburban. Rachel thought she saw a tear on his cheek. "Are you okay, Dad?"

"Oh, yes, my girl. We're following the star, aren't we? I couldn't be better." Joe navigated and Peter drove carefully, following directions. Polaris guided them straight through the frozen fields, past the shimmering lake, and onto Old Oak Lane—just the road Peter had been looking for.

No sooner had they reached Old Oak Lane than the sky mysteriously clouded over and Polaris disappeared. Huge snowflakes returned and danced wildly on the windshield, artfully dodging each swipe of the wipers. They forced Peter to slow the Suburban to a crawl.

"Hurry, Daddy, hurry," Lizzy pleaded. "We've got to get there before it's too late!" She was anxious to deliver their gathered Christmas.

"Now, where is the blasted place?" Peter couldn't see a thing, but the darkness was somehow slowly growing brighter. They rounded the bend and everyone saw it at once—the magical, miraculous star! As the road curved slightly to the east, out of the fog and falling snowflakes the brilliant, silvery star shone majestically above the humble trailer park.

"By golly! We've found our star." Grandpa Joe blinked in amazement. "Or maybe it has found us," he mumbled to himself. Peter stopped the Suburban to look at the star.

The lighted star above the old trailer park seemed oddly out of place in these surroundings, like a sparkling stone lost from an expensive piece of jewelry and left here by its unknowing owner, waiting to be rediscovered.

The star itself was carved from hardwood and polished to a fine luster. It stretched to a height of nearly six feet at its apex and extended nearly the same width. The carving gave the appearance of overlapping triangles with additional points of light reaching out from every edge and point. Curiously, the star was lighted by hundreds of brilliant white Christmas tree lights brought through carefully drilled holes and placed just shy of the polished surface so that the star appeared to glow from within, creating its own source of brightness. Curiously, the lights faded in and out, giving the same undulating luminosity as a twinkling constellation. The placement of this "Winter Star" upon the dark hilly outcropping above the park made it appear to actually join the other stars in the heavens. In fact, in the early evening, from a distance, the star appeared to rise on the horizon, beckoning weary travelers to the humble accommodations below.

"I've never seen anything like it. And it's in the middle of nowhere," Rachel commented.

"I don't get it," Sara whispered. "It's eerie, if you ask me."

Lizzy just stared at the enormous star.

Paul, as usual, spewed a stream of questions. "Hey, where did that come from? How come it's so bright. What is it for?"

"It's a sign," Peter said.

Rachel smiled at her husband and thought how wonderful it was that Peter was so caught up in the Christmas spirit. "You're right, Peter. It's a sign of Christmas and of goodness and of hope in a dark world. A new star in the sky—it's a sign of love and sacrifice and everything good that's going to happen from this point on in our lives. Like a new beginning, a new birth." Rachel looked at Peter, believing that he must be feeling her joy. For him to recognize this as a sign from above—that must mean that he too felt like God was communicating with them in a mysterious way. After all, this whole night had been extremely mysterious. She leaned her head on his shoulder as they sat and watched the star. Silence surrounded them, and Rachel sang softly, "Silent night, holy night." Everyone joined her song. "All is calm, all is bright . . ." They sang the whole song—all three verses.

"What I was trying to say, though I hate to admit it now and spoil the spirit, is that this star is really a sign," Peter tried to explain.

"I know it is, Peter, and because of this sign we'll be better—"

"No, I mean it's a *sign* sign. You know, on a wooden post, built by some construction worker—a real, honest-to-goodness sign. See, on its base it has the name of the trailer park where Santa's family lives."

The snow and mist had cleared enough now that everyone could see that Peter was right—there was a post holding up the star-sign. "Starlight Trailer Court" appeared at the base of the pole, neatly painted in fancy blue letters.

Grandpa Joe hopped out of the Suburban. He hurried to the post and ran his hand over the sign's lettering as if he were caressing a long-lost friend. With his binoculars he inspected the post, the star, and the sign. The others watched.

"What are you doing, Grampa?" Paul called from his rolled-down window. Grandpa Joe didn't answer.

Peter jumped out and joined Joe. "What is it, Joe?"

"Oh, it's nothing. I just thought I recognized something, but I was wrong." He pointed to the bottom right-hand corner of the lettering, where he'd brushed the snow away. It was signed, "Orion."

Peter looked at Joe's eyes. He had seen this same disappointment on Rachel's face a hundred times. It was the look she wore when she thought that Joey was going to succeed or that he was going to quit using, or that he was going to come to Thanksgiving or Christmas, but then he didn't. Funny, though, this look used to anger Peter. Tonight it didn't. *Maybe that star's changing me,* he thought. He put his arm around Joseph and led him back to the Suburban.

Even Peter decided to believe that their star had led them to a new place. He started to hope that divine intervention had actually occurred. Peter Stone suddenly began to feel what it meant to never stop hoping.

Offering

Santa's plan worked wonderfully. The girls replaced the nametags on each gift as Peter parked the Suburban a ways away from the designated trailer house. Peter, David, Paul, and Joe then sneaked, gifts in hand, toward their destination. The girls stayed inside the Suburban, where they had an unobstructed view of the front porch. They were watching to warn the men if anyone approached.

Sneaking up the icy wooden steps was not an easy task. Peter's foot slipped and down he went. Presents scattered, but the boys hurried to gather them. A neighbor's dog barked loudly and bounded toward them. It growled and bared his sharp teeth, but when Paul pulled a piece of old beef jerky out of his coat pocket, the fierce enemy wagged its tail and became a trusting ally.

They piled the presents neatly on the porch and turned to leave. Too late! The porch light clicked on, the front door opened, and the delivery boys were trapped.

They stood there looking guilty—like naughty children caught stealing bubble gum. They didn't know how the man would react to their presence.

Awkward silence surrounded them, but then the kind man smiled. "Well, whaddaya know! Looks like Santa's found us after all." He called his wife to come and meet his new friends. He opened the tattered screen door and ushered them inside his humble home. The living room was neat and tidy. The furnishings were well used but warm and inviting. In the corner stood a tiny Christmas tree without a single present beneath it. The man's wife entered, carrying a plate of warm cookies. She offered the cookies to the visitors, and Paul and David ate theirs in one gulp.

Paul was the first to speak. "How did you know that Santa sent us?"

The man grinned. "Just a good guess, I suppose. Please, have a seat." Peter and Grandpa Joe each found a place to sit, while David hurriedly piled the presents around the Christmas tree and then plopped down on the couch.

Only Paul remained standing. "Santa really did send us," he declared. "He came to our house tonight and told us about the airport thing and how you had to move out of your house, and how his elves forgot—"

"Paul!" David interrupted, stopping his brother mid-sentence.

The man looked inquisitively back and forth from Joe to Peter. His wife did the same. And their children could now be seen peeking shyly around the corner.

"It's true," Peter confirmed. "Santa sent us. We are just his messengers bearing these humble gifts. We sincerely hope that you will accept these offerings and have a Merry Christmas." Peter motioned toward the lovely pile of gifts.

The man's wife studied their faces. "Do we know you?" she asked.

"No, you don't," Peter answered. "And we don't know you. But somehow Santa knows us all."

"Santa knows everyone," a small, raspy voice squeaked from behind the rocking chair.

"That's Beth, our youngest daughter," the mother explained.

Everyone laughed, and Grandpa Joe reached for another cookie. His hunger had caught up with him when he smelled the warm cookies, and he regretted that he hadn't eaten dinner with the rest of the family.

Peter and the boys enjoyed their short visit. By now, the children had appeared—all except Beth, that is. The tiny child with the adorable voice stayed safely tucked away behind the rocking chair.

Joe stood abruptly. "We won't keep you any longer. We've got to be going." Peter, David, and Paul started toward the door. They wished Santa's forgotten family a Merry Christmas, and the family's gratitude was obvious.

The woman gave Grandpa Joe two more cookies and a kiss on the cheek. "Thank you. You brought us Christmas. How can we ever repay you?"

Peter and the boys were on the porch with the man, but Joe paused inside to gather a bit of information. "That star sign—can you tell me where it came from?"

The woman's face melted into softness. "Oh, yes! Isn't it beautiful? One of the renters here, a wonderful man named Orion who lives at the end of our street, designed and built it himself. He's an artist and a carpenter. We were all very much amazed when we saw it. We had a ceremony and lit it for the first time a few weeks ago—on Thanksgiving night. We lit candles and talked about the things we are thankful for in our lives. Most of us here have very little, but I wish you could have heard the expressions of love and gratitude that were shared. Our star united us and inspired us to clean up and redo our streets, homes, and, in some cases, ourselves in Starlight Trailer Park. Isn't it incredible that one star could make such a difference?"

"My thoughts, precisely. Incredible."

Grandpa Joe thanked the woman and left. Once outside, he looked through his binoculars for a clearer view of Orion's trailer at the end of the street. It was small and white, with a gray, wooden porch. A nicely placed little pine tree stood in a terra-cotta pot on the porch, and a few white Christmas lights twinkled from its evergreen branches.

Peter and the boys headed for the Suburban, and the man walked Joe to the street.

"Do you know the star-builder, Orion?" Joe asked him without moving from behind his binoculars.

The man grinned. "Oh, you bet I do. He's a great guy. He and his cute wife have been cleaning up this place. It was really a dump before they came last September. He started planning our star clear back then. He showed us drawings of it. Then he showed us drawings of what he envisioned this trailer park could be with some work. He got us all together and inspired us. None of us believed it was possible to make such an enormous change, but Orion said that change is never easy, but that he knew it could be done. He said it with such conviction that we knew he was right. We believed him. And as you can see, he was correct."

Joe surveyed the area. The trailer park was as neat as a pin. Joseph could see that beneath the snow, every picket fence had been freshly mended and painted. The outside of each trailer was in top shape. The porches were all brand new, and lining the sidewalks were terra-cotta pots all holding small living evergreens with twinkling white Christmas lights.

The man noticed Joseph's gaze resting on the trees. "The owner says it's the first time he ever remembers this place with Christmas trees and lights," he commented.

Grandpa Joe looked up toward the enormous star. "Where does the dark go when the light comes?" The man looked at Joe inquisitively. "Just something my grandson taught me," Grandpa Joe explained. "I best be hurrying now. Christmas is coming." As he hurried back to the Suburban, Joe decided that he would visit Starlight Trailer Park again.

* * *

Late Summer 1990

"This place could actually be pretty funky—I mean picture everything cleaned up and painted . . . and maybe some planters along the street. A little paint and some elbow grease and we could create quite a sweet-lookin' neighborhood." Orion spoke with confidence. He was an artist and a carpenter, and he knew exactly what it would take to spruce up the dilapidated old trailer park.

His petite wife, Annie, stood beside him surveying their street. Annie was in her last year at Summit City College, where she was majoring in landscape design. She loved planting seeds and watching them grow. While most people hated weeding, Annie thoroughly enjoyed it. She said it gave her hope to see a freshly weeded and fertilized flower bed. Knowing that her plants would be able to flourish and share their beauty gave her great satisfaction.

September was Annie's favorite time of year. The plants were in full bloom and summer was coming to a close, bringing sunshine and cool breezes.

Annie faced Orion. "This is really exciting." She put her hand in his. "I can hardly wait to see it when we're finished. Do you really think we can do it?"

"What? My Annie, the one who believes that I can do anything, doubting me even for a minute?"

"Oh, no, I'm not doubting you, my good husband," she teased. "I'm just wondering, no, I'm hoping we can get it all finished before the first snowfall."

"I say Thanksgiving and we'll have this place looking like a million bucks. I know you, Annie. When you set out on a project, you don't quit until you're satisfied." His grin softened into a look of sincere appreciation. "I know. I was one of your projects once."

They shared a knowing look, then Annie pretended to punch him in the stomach. "I know a good thing when I see it, that's all—even if it is a bit rusty and beat-up on the outside. Besides, you had nearly completed yourself by the time I met you. You just needed a little sprucing up inside and a lot of love to make you blossom into the man I know and love. Anyhow, I like to concentrate on what's underneath. You know, it's what's underneath that really matters, right?"

Orion suddenly swooped his little wife off her feet and twirled her around. As he hugged her tightly, he laughed and kissed her forehead. "Good thing for me that you saw something worthwhile here." He set her down carefully and grinned boyishly. "Cuz we all know how 'rusty' I was when you first found me."

"But underneath, you sparkled like a star."

"Really? You really saw a sparkle? Wow. You're good. I didn't think I had any sparkle left in me."

She smiled. "So when do we start? I can see hydrangeas here, red weigela in each corner, flowering plum trees equally spaced at each driveway, and oh, Orion, let's make a hundred terra-cotta planters, plant a little spruce in each, and then fill in around them with perennials—deep red sweet william and carnations. Oh, and roses—red and white roses everywhere we can fit them in. Let's fix up all the porches and the fences and paint them gray and white. All the neighbors will help. I know they will, and—"

"Slow down, Annie. We need to start with a plan. I'll draw it up tonight, and tomorrow we can take it around to all the neighbors and see what they think."

Orion was so anxious that he stayed up all night, planning and sketching his ideas: Flower beds in the shape of stars. Every couple of hours, he whispered Annie awake to show her. She loved every idea he had, and she expressed her groggy delight each time he awakened her.

"That's lovely . . . a white star-shaped rose garden in the middle of the entry street. You'd better get some sleep, honey. You'll get sick if you don't." Then she'd fall asleep and Orion would go back to his drafting desk. Trellises and picket fences filled the Starlight Trailer Park drawings. He finished with beautiful terra-cotta planters lining the streets just as Annie had envisioned. Then he designed the magnificent star sign. He couldn't wait another second. At exactly seven A.M. he woke Annie and pulled her out of bed. He wrapped her in her yellow robe and fixed orange juice and wheat toast—no butter, just the way she liked it. Then he led her to the little kitchen table. She rubbed her eyes and blinked away the sleep. The drawings were exquisite! She was thrilled.

Showering and dressing took way too long, but then they were out the door, rousting out the neighbors. Every single neighbor caught the vision—how could they help but join in the overly enthusiastic couple's dreams? Every neighbor had some talent or trade to contribute.

"Count on us. We'll help every step of the way. My wife's a great painter, and I'm pretty good at wood-working," the Stirlands said excitedly.

The Nelsens were a very friendly couple with four darling children. They had lost their home just a few weeks before, so they were excited to see someone clean up the old trailer park. "When do we start? I love to plant anything, but especially roses. Before the airport expansion took our home, I had a gorgeous rose garden—red is my favorite. And Daniel just loves to grow trees. Ours were the tallest and the straightest in our old neighborhood."

Similar responses came from every family in the park, and everyone agreed to begin early Saturday morning

"Orion," Annie whispered, "your drawings are what sold everyone. You know that, right?"

"Well, I think maybe your ideas on the plantings had a lot to do with it."

"We make a good team, husband."

"Yes, we do, wife."

Orion and Annie liked to call each other by their still-new titles. They had been married only one year. But they swore that they'd still like their "husband" and "wife" titles even when they had been married sixty years.

Orion was exhausted as the sun set on the Starlight Trailer Park that evening. Annie sat beside him on their rickety little porch steps. They liked to sit together each evening and look at the stars—from outside when it was warm enough and from inside when it wasn't. Orion stretched out and laid his head on his wife's lap. He commented that her lap was growing smaller as her tummy grew bigger. Their baby was due just after Christmas. Annie caressed Orion's messy blond hair . . . actually, she never referred to it as messy. She said it had character and a mind of its own, just like Orion.

They watched the stars quietly. After a while Orion mumbled softly, "Will you say prayer tonight, hon? I'm so tired."

She bent down and kissed each of his now-closed eyes. "Yes, I'd like to say our prayer tonight."

Annie spoke with God, as she did every morning and night, much the same as she talked with everyone she loved—peacefully and faithfully. She talked and then listened and then talked some more. When she finally closed her prayer and said amen, she did not expect a response from Orion. She figured he had drifted away at the very beginning. But to her surprise, Orion had listened to every word of her sweet prayer. He knew that faith, God, and lots of work were what had pulled him through his darkest hours. So when she said she was grateful, she spoke for both of them.

* * *

Christmas Eve Night 1990

"Tell us everything, every detail," Rachel pleaded, beaming.

Peter recounted the events of their "anonymous" Christmas Eve visit—vicious dog, beef jerky, and all, for the girls—and Grandpa Joe climbed into the Suburban just in time to hear the telling of the last details.

"So they were happy?" Lizzy asked with a giggle.

David assured her that the children were very happy. Lizzy and Paul snuggled up together in the back of the Suburban.

"They didn't have any presents Liz—none at all," Paul added. "Ours were all they got."

Lizzy looked at her brother earnestly. "I'm glad we gave them our presents, aren't you?"

But Paul was too sleepy to answer her, and she was too tired to care.

They drove straight home. Rachel thought it was worth noting that their trip home was much shorter than the journey there had been. Peter pulled into the garage and then carried Lizzy and Paul to their beds. Joe headed for his pick-up.

"Where on earth are you going, Dad?" Rachel asked, following him back outside. "You're staying here tonight, aren't you?"

"I'll be back, Rach. I've got a couple of things I need to do first." Joe was filled with excitement and emotion. "Don't set the alarm. I'm sure it will be late when I get finished."

"But Dad, do you know it's after eleven? You really shouldn't be out in this weather. It's supposed to get pretty snowy around midnight, and the roads are going to be really slick!"

"I know, I know. I'll be careful. Don't worry." He waved off her concerns and hurried to his truck.

Peter opened the front door from inside and beckoned his wife back into the house. "Where is your dad going? He really worries me sometimes."

Rachel gave him a confused look. "I don't have any idea. He's got something planned, though. I could see it in his eyes."

Rachel and Peter readied everything for Christmas morning. Rachel already had everything prepared; they just needed to arrange it all. She had even pre-made the sweet rolls and put them in the fridge, ready to go into the oven first thing in the morning.

Joe knew what he wanted to accomplish. He wondered as he drove if he would be able to find his way back to the Starlight Trailer Park. He really hoped that the star sign would still be lit.

He pulled his truck into his own garage and bustled inside his house. He went straight to his linen closet and grabbed a white sheet, then headed for the newest of his two telescopes. He loved this telescope. He had purchased it last year when it had finally been marked down during an after-Christmas clearance sale downtown. It was the nicest scope he had ever been able to afford. It could find things automatically. It was almost as nice as Rachel's. You simply calibrated it and then punched in the name of what you wished to see and it would accurately move itself. Wonderful, modern convenience.

Without hesitating, Joe wrapped it carefully in the sheet and then carried it to his truck. He positioned it on the seat next to him, and then fastened a seat belt around the precious cargo. He drove eastward in silence. Thankfully, the sky stayed clear and the star was visible, so he was able to remain on the paved road during the entire journey.

His thoughts were a mixture of trepidation and joy. Would his offering be well received? Or would he be rejected? Suddenly, he was beneath the star. He turned off his headlights and crept along Starlight Trailer Park's tidy little street. He passed the home of Santa's forgotten family. Except for the star sign, there was no light at all. Even the lights on the little evergreens had retired for a long winter's nap.

He stopped, got out, and sneaked around to the side of Orion's little trailer. He heard a dog bark, and he hoped that he wouldn't be detected twice in one night by the same fierce canine.

He tiptoed through the snow to the window and peeked inside.

The trailer was an eclectic mixture of art studio, planetarium, and home. Every inch was specially designed to provide both comfort and economy of space. In one corner a miniature woodworking shop included built-in cabinets handsomely carved from a varied collection of woods, complete with raised panels and a metal countertop. The shop even included suspended power tools hanging from cabinets above.

In the opposite corner was the planetarium, with its own secondhand telescope positioned in to a custom-created bay window that resembled a miniature glass-room greenhouse—plant seedlings in paper cups lined the glass on all sides. A small stool on wheels sat between the carpenter shop and the planetarium.

Separating the planetarium and the shop was a tiny art studio with a variety of sketches and watercolors. They were displayed on an easel suspended from the ceiling. The walls were covered with star charts, Hubble telescope pictures of the universe, and a myriad of constellation sketches. The room radiated energy, genius, shape, form, and an irresistible sense of wonder with nature and the universe.

Joe smiled and stepped back from the window, letting out a contented sigh. It was exactly as he had suspected: Orion was a stargazer! Joe would never stop hoping.

Waiting

Christmas Eve Night 1990

Joe hurried back to his truck and retrieved the telescope. "I hope you enjoy your new home," he whispered, cradling the device in his arms. Had anyone been watching, they would have been certain that the old man had just abandoned a snugly wrapped baby on the little gray porch. Joe paused only a moment before rushing back to his truck and driving away. The last things he remembered were the blinding snow and his frantic attempts to avoid the huge power pole that had appeared out of nowhere in the blizzard.

When he opened his eyes, he was startled to say the least. The lights were too bright and the pain in his head pulsed on and off. He tried to sit up, but dizziness overcame him. He struggled to free himself from the straps that held him captive. Panic seized him.

A woman dressed in green smiled down at him. Her red hair was a lovely shade, he thought, and the light created a soft halo around her head. "Where am I?" Joe mumbled.

"Don't worry, sir, you're in good hands now. You had a bit of an auto accident, I'm afraid. You're at Valley Hospital Emergency Room. I'm your nurse, and my name is Liberty Taylor. Now let me look at this ugly cut on your head." The pretty nurse spoke as she cleaned Joseph's wound. "Dr. Thomas is your doctor, and I assure you, though his bedside manner leaves a lot to be desired, he is actually a very skilled physician. I promise you we will take good care of you." She paused and seemed to notice the change in his expression. "I'll bet you'd like to know how you got here, right?"

"That thought was just occurring to me."

"Can you sit up just a bit and look out into the receiving area?" She helped him sit up, and he saw a room full of what appeared to be very tattered street people. "Do you see the Santa over by the door?" she asked. He surveyed the room and saw three, no four Santa's, and they all looked like the Santa who had visited the Stone home earlier—they all had the same magnificent red suits.

He blinked long and hard. "I see several Santas!"

"Well, it is Christmas Eve, you know."

"You mean one of them brought me here?" For the second time in one night, Joseph realized he had been rescued by Saint Nicholas.

"Yes. The Santa by the door found you on the side of the road. He could see you weren't hurt too badly, so he loaded you into his van, which was nearly full of homeless people that he had picked up near where he found you. He was bringing them here to receive medical attention, so he figured you'd fit right in—not with the homeless, I mean, just with the sick or injured. It's part of an elaborate plan these Santas have to get free medical attention for the needy. They're the only ones I've ever seen actually succeed in convincing Dr. Thomas to give his attention to sick people without first making sure they were insured. Then they got it all on the news. It's actually very clever, don't you think?"

Joe stared at all of the people. "Do these guys masquerade like this and bring homeless people here often?"

"Only on Christmas Eve." Liberty winked and then left him to check on the reporters and TV cameras in the receiving room. As she parted the curtain, she came face to face with a TV camera. Joseph smiled and waved. He assumed he had just made the late news. He was correct.

* * *

"Rachel! Rachel, come quick. It's your dad!"

Rachel hurried into their family room. "Oh good, he's home," she exclaimed.

"No, look! He's on television . . . at the hospital, I think."

Rachel caught just a glimpse of Joseph as he lay on the hospital gurney, holding his bleeding head. "We've got to go to him, Peter. You grab the kids; we can't leave them here alone. I'll pull out the Suburban."

Peter prodded his sleeping children from their beds and instructed them to grab their blankets and slippers. He then rushed them outside and into the waiting Suburban.

"I'd better drive, Rach. The snow's pretty bad."

"You're right." She jumped out and hurried to the passenger side. "Everybody buckle up. We're going to the hospital to get Grandpa Joe."

The kids were too groggy to consider that their grandfather might be in serious condition. They were simply thrilled to participate in such a wonderful Christmas Eve adventure.

"Is Grampa okay?" Paul asked.

"Yes, at least he looked like it on TV," Rachel answered.

"Cool, how'd he get to be on TV, Dad?"

"We have no idea, son. It was the late news. It looked in part like a tag from an earlier story. It said something about a good doctor who had spent Christmas Eve treating the homeless for free. It also said the homeless people had been brought to the hospital by four incredible Santas. It showed an earlier clip of them and they looked exactly like the Santa who visited us tonight."

"No kidding, Dad?" David was clearly impressed. He thought of how much work Santa was doing on Christmas Eve. "I wonder what else old St. Nick has done tonight."

"Can't believe it myself, David. Saint Nicholas is certainly in good form tonight, isn't he?"

Lizzy giggled. "Oh yes, Daddy. Santa Claus is always in good form—especially on Christmas Eve."

"Drive safely, Peter," Rachel cautioned worriedly. "We don't want anything else to go wrong. I sure hope Dad's okay."

Finally, Peter pulled up at the ER entrance to Valley Hospital. "You guys hop out here," he said. "I'll park and be right in."

The Stone children, clad in their new Christmas pajamas, piled out of the Suburban and hurried through the emergency entrance. The doors opened automatically and the smell of sterilized air filled the night air. Lizzy held her nose and commented on the unpleasant odor.

A pretty, red-headed nurse greeted them with a pleasant but weary smile. The waiting area was mostly empty now. There was not a sign of any huge crowd of homeless patients and no visible clue that Santa—or rather, several Santas—had visited earlier.

Paul noticed something red on the floor near the registration desk. He ran over and picked it up. "Hey, look guys! This red glove is exactly like the one Santa forgot at our house!"

Rachel immediately rummaged through her coat pocket. She pulled out their red glove. A perfect match.

Peter raised his eyebrows. "Now that's what I call a sign."

Rachel laughed and kissed him on the cheek.

"May I help you?" the red-headed nurse asked. "You don't look too sick, especially in your Christmas jammies," she teased.

David and Sara felt a bit self-conscious, but Paul and Lizzy were proud to be sporting their new pj's.

"We're not sick, silly," Lizzy explained. "We're just looking for Santa Claus."

"She means Grandpa Joe," Paul corrected.

"Have you seen him?" Rachel looked anxious.

"Santa?" The nurse winked.

"No, my father. Oh, I'm sorry." Rachel slowed down. "We saw my dad on the news . . . and, well . . . we've come to get him—if he's okay, that is. His name is Joseph Keller. His head was bleeding, and he's an older man—mostly bald, blue eyes, can be sort of ornery."

"Oh, I do remember him. He'd been in an accident . . . said his truck slid off the road and into a power pole by the lake. One of our Santas brought him in." She looked through the papers on her clipboard. "Yes, here he is. Dr. Thomas treated him for a forehead laceration. He left here a while ago."

Rachel couldn't believe he'd already left. "Who did he leave with? He had nothing to drive!" she exclaimed.

"You know, I really didn't notice who he was with, but I don't think he was alone. It seems to me that . . . um . . .

yes . . . could he have been with a very pregnant woman in a blue coat? Yes . . . I believe I saw him helping a pregnant woman. They—"

"He left with a pregnant woman who was wearing a blue coat?" Peter repeated her words, hoping he had misunderstood.

"Yes. I'm sure they walked out together. I asked if he needed a ride, but he said no. I remember thinking it was sort of odd because they went outside and looked at the sky. He was pointing upward and showing her something."

"That's got to be Dad. Where could he have gone?"

"Your family has always been weird, Rach, but this takes the cake. I have no idea what's going on." Normally, Peter would have been furious—traipsing around the country in the middle of night—on Christmas Eve of all nights—but all he felt was calm and peace. In fact, since the star, he had felt no anger whatsoever. Could it be a miracle?

* * *

Christmas Eve Night 1990

"Are you sure it's time, Annie?" Orion jumped out of bed and frantically ran for his coat. "But the baby's not due for two more weeks. How can this be? Is the hospital open on Christmas Eve? Oh, of course it is." Orion was talking as fast as his thoughts were coming, sputtering anything and everything that passed through his mind.

"Yes, I'm certain it's time. Could you help me with my suitcase? And you may want to put on some clothes besides your coat." Annie was lugging her own bag toward the door.

"Don't you dare lift that! We don't want anything to go wrong now—not after waiting so long for this kid to get

here." He grabbed Annie's bag and helped her down the back steps.

"It looks like we may get a Christmas present tomorrow after all." They had agreed a few months before that rather than getting gifts for one another, they would use their money to buy the Christmas lights for the trailer park. Now they were about to be repaid for their sacrifice.

"You're going to be a daddy! Can you believe it?" Annie was trembling with excitement and, of course, fear as they drove along the snowy road toward the hospital. Her pains weren't unbearable, but they were increasing as they traveled. After what seemed an incredibly lengthy ride, Orion pulled the truck into the ER entrance at Valley Hospital.

"I'm going to let you out here." Orion was now in control and thinking clearly. "I'll park the truck and be right in. Will you be okay until I get back?"

"I'll be fine. I think we've still got a little while anyway. But then, I've never done this before, so I don't really know what to expect." Annie was half-joking but mostly serious as she moved toward the ER entrance. Orion blew her a kiss and hurried away. Once inside, she was overtaken with fear. Tears stung her eyes. She swiped at them, hoping no one had noticed, and told herself it was just her crazy emotions trying to get the better of her. She felt alone and afraid without Orion.

* * *

Joseph Keller signed the hospital papers, which relieved the hospital of its responsibility for him (he was leaving the hospital AMA—against medical advice). The nurse explained to him all the symptoms he should watch out for and which ones would necessitate his return to the hospital. She asked if he needed a ride somewhere, but he said he didn't. He headed toward the pay phone near the entry but stopped abruptly when he saw the petite woman with the bulging stomach and teary eyes.

"May I help you?" He smiled and offered her his arm. Normally, he wouldn't have even noticed the young woman, but tonight he was different. He was full of what he believed was Christmas spirit, and he really wanted to reach out to her.

Normally she wouldn't have accepted help from a strange man, but tonight she was different too. She gladly accepted. She certainly didn't feel like being alone, and she was oddly drawn to the kind-looking gentleman, so she took his arm.

"Thank you . . . I . . . um . . . I don't really know where to go. I'm looking for the . . ."

"The baby birthing place?" He looked into her eyes for approval.

"Yes . . . exactly. But how did you know?"

He deliberately stared at her stomach, then back into her eyes. She held her enormous stomach and laughed at herself. Joseph laughed with her. He wanted to comfort her and to help her. These feelings were so foreign to him. While they laughed he suddenly had what he thought was a brilliant idea. He held her hand under his arm and led her outside.

She was so touched by his kindness and comforted by his compassion that she willingly accompanied him.

"Wearing that blue coat and looking so young and so frightened, you remind me of someone. Look—over there against the horizon. Do you see it? Can you see the new star? It reminds me of the Christ Child's star. Your baby . . ."

Annie squinted her eyes and followed where he was pointing. She was amazed!

"You can see it from clear over here?" Now her emotions were out of control. She was crying uncontrollably, and Joseph pulled a clean white hankie out of his pocket and handed it to her. She wiped her face and tried to speak. "That's my star. Orion built it for me."

Joseph stared at her in disbelief. "You? Orion built that star for you? You are Orion's wife?" He was now crying with her, and she shared his hankie with him. "And this is Orion's baby?" Joseph's thoughts were running circles in his brain. "But how can this be? This is a miracle!"

They stood together a moment longer. Annie had lots of questions, but she was instantly overcome with the worst pain she had felt thus far. She groaned and doubled over. Joseph caught her just in time.

"We've got to get you to the baby place. Nurse!" he called. "Please, we need a wheelchair." A tall, skinny brunette nurse hurried over, and they helped Annie into the chair. The nurse pushed and Joseph hurried alongside asking lots of questions. "So, what is your name?"

"Annie . . ." She couldn't finish. The pain was too bad.

Joseph waited anxiously for the pain to pass. Then he asked more questions, stealing away any chance for her to say anything except answer him.

"Where is Orion?"

"Parking the truck."

"And how long have you been married to Orion?"

"A little over a year."

"So this is your first child?"

"Of course."

"Do you know if you're having a boy or girl?"

101

"Boy."

"And have you chosen a name for him?"

"Yes." Another pain came hard. Annie didn't continue.

"Well, what is it, Annie? What is your son's name to be?" Joseph was oddly anxious.

The nurse shot Joseph a frown, apparently frustrated with his merciless interrogation. "Sir, this girl is in labor. She doesn't want to answer any more of your silly questions."

Annie actually wanted him to be there. She knew it seemed strange, but she really liked him. Somehow she felt comfortable with him. He was curiously familiar to her, and she wanted him to stay.

"Oh, I'm so sorry!" Joseph realized what he'd done, and he sincerely apologized. He stepped away from the moving wheelchair.

Annie reached out and grabbed his arm. "Please don't leave." Tears streamed down her pale face, and Joseph held onto her hand. He was so glad to know that for whatever reason, she didn't want him to leave. He looked at the nurse, who gave him a dirty look, and then repeated his last question.

"So what are you planning to name him?"

"We've decided on . . . Joseph . . . after his . . . father."

This time the impatient nurse interrupted. "But I thought you said your husband's name was Orion."

"Yes . . . it is." She waited for the pain to pass. The nurse raised her eyebrows, shook her head, and looked at Joseph.

Annie breathed deeply and then tried to explain. "You see, my husband changed his name a while ago—not legally, just personally. He had lived a rather colorful life before, but then he had decided to change. To do that, he had to change everything—his thinking, his behavior, and his relationship with God. He became a new person. He chose the name Orion because he said his father would like that, and he wanted to be something his father could be proud of again."

"Joseph is a good name. In fact, that's my name." Annie looked up at him in wonder. She was figuring out exactly what he had ascertained earlier that evening at the trailer park.

Joseph stopped the wheelchair and knelt down to her eye level. "Orion is Joey—Joseph Keller, Jr.—isn't he? And you are my daughter-in-law."

Annie was stunned. She studied Joseph's face as she put everything together in her mind. "But how? I mean . . . where? . . . Oh my!" She doubled over in pain. "So how did you know who I am? We've never met."

"I had no idea who you were. When I saw you come into the hospital in your present state, wearing that blue coat, you made me think of Mary, the mother of Jesus. And I was overcome with admiration for you. I allowed myself to feel something, which I normally don't do, and I wanted to help you. I wanted to know you and to somehow be a part of your life and the life of your baby. It was the strangest feeling I've ever had. You were a complete stranger, and I thought you would turn me away. But I didn't worry about that, and you didn't. You welcomed me, so I showed you the star, but you already knew the star. It's your star. When I saw that you knew the star, then I believed I knew you."

The gruff nurse pushed the chair forward. "This family reunion is very touching, but we've got another member of this family that's about to show up, so let's get moving here, people.

* * *

With the nurse's gruff dismissal, Joe reluctantly released his grasp on Annie's hand. Annie looked back over her shoulder at him until the doors to the maternity ward swung shut behind her and blocked him from her sight. Joe had never done the hospital thing well. He found the maternity waiting room and then paced and fidgeted. He had never been able to take stressful situations sitting down. And so he paced and thought and paced some more.

The maternity waiting room was lonely and desolate. A few three-month-old magazines were neatly stacked on a coffee table next to rows of empty wooden chairs. At the far end of the waiting room, cold, dark windows stretched from floor to ceiling. The storm outside had resumed, taking new strength from the lake effect, and heavy snowflakes scurried southward, driven by a brisk wind. In the background on a small television suspended from the ceiling, Joe could barely make out the last scene from *It's a Wonderful Life*—the scene where George Bailey greets all his friends who trusted him and rallied around him in his time of need. Jimmy Stewart was saying something about the angel, Clarence, getting his wings, when Joe found his own reflection in the darkened waiting room windows. He looked at himself carefully, examining the old man before him. On closer inspection, he couldn't help noticing that his reflection stood surrounded by a fierce tempest. He felt as if he had been captured in a miniature snow scene—the kind that creates an artificial flurry of snow when shaken. His life, along with the scene around him, was being shaken, and he was jarred into a sense of responsibility and action.

He looked at his reflection again, wanting to ask the old man why he had disowned his son. Why, unlike Rachel, he had lost all hope. Why he had given up on his own flesh and blood. If given the chance to beg forgiveness, would his son accept Joseph as his father or would Joseph too be disowned?

Now he began to scold himself. "How could you be so cold, heartless, and unforgiving? Look at all you've lost, old fool—a beautiful daughter-in-law, another grandchild soon to be born. Was your anger and your selfishness so important, old man?" Joseph couldn't bear to look at his reflection in the window any longer. He dropped his gaze to the floor. In the background he heard the words to "Auld Lang Syne" playing softly as *It's a Wonderful Life* concluded. Joe muttered to himself, "It *could* have been a wonderful life."

* * *

Joey immediately recognized the man in the window. He stood almost next to his father; their reflections touched shoulders and elbows in the dark glass before them. The older Joseph, head still bowed, hadn't noticed that his son now stood beside him. A thousand thoughts raced through Joey's mind. "Would he, could he ever forgive me? How can I ever make up for all the heartache I have caused?" How does one ask forgiveness for breaking hearts, and for causing disappointment and despair beyond repair?

Joe's thoughts mingled with Joey's, " Oh where does the love go when the hate comes? Is it possible that love can swallow hatred?"

The old man raised his eyes to the reflection in the window and was startled to find another person there. He blinked and upon opening his eyes again recognized an older and transformed version of his long-lost son standing next to him.

They both spoke at once. Joe begged for forgiveness for losing hope and for hating, and he pleaded to make up for time lost. Joey spoke over his father, begging him for another chance to make up for the pain he had caused. Breathless in their exchange, they paused, looking into one another's eyes. They embraced as the tears flowed freely. Joey slumped into the strength of his father's shoulders and sobbed like a small child. With a meager attempt at composure, Joe explained, as he still held his son, that he had found the Winter Star and that he had followed it to Joey's home. He explained that the telescope that now lay on Joey's porch was an offering of peace and love. Finally, he explained that his search for the star had eventually led him to Joey's beautiful bride, Annie. Like a wise man from times past, he had followed the star and found hope for repentance and forgiveness in a newborn child. Forgiveness—a marvelous, magical gift from God.

Eager to reunite Joey with the rest of the family, Joe immediately invited his son to join them all on New Year's Eve. "By then, your son will be ready to meet his whole family. You know how it works, Joey. The fun and games begin in the afternoon around two, and dinner will start at six thirty. You can still find Rachel's home, can't you?"

Joey looked once again into his father's tear-streaked eyes and found what he had searched so long to find: not only forgiveness, but also love. As they embraced again, they heard someone hurry into the waiting room.

"Is there an Orion Keller in here?" a nurse in Dr. Seuss–print scrubs called into the waiting room.

Joey instantly stiffened with nervousness and pulled away from his father. "Uh, right here!" he replied.

The nurse smiled and hurried over to him. "Well if you want to be with your wife when your baby is born, I suggest you come with me. Babies can't be kept waiting, you know!"

* * *

"Peter, where could he have gone?" Rachel didn't know what to do.

"And what pregnant woman was he stargazing with?" Peter was trying to think but not making any sense of the information they had just received.

"I think we should get back home, Rachel. Maybe he'll try to call us."

"Didn't you bring your cell phone?"

"No. Didn't you bring yours?"

She shook her head. "Okay," she reluctantly agreed.

"Let's go, everyone. Bundle up. It's a bit of a walk." Peter helped everyone wrap themselves, and the puzzled family set out for home.

* * *

New Year's Eve 1990

The holidays were the happiest the Stone family had experienced in six years. Santa had delivered help, and the star that led them all to reach out to someone in need had brought change. Rachel and Peter quit fighting, and even

Grandpa Joe was a new man. His accident had turned out to be small, and everyone was grateful for that. When he finally returned on Christmas morning, he was somewhat elusive about where he had spent the night, but he seemed happier than ever. He spent nearly the whole time between Christmas and New Year's at the Stone home with his family.

New Year's Eve was yet another traditional family gathering. Rachel looked forward to it almost as much as she did Thanksgiving and Christmas, and like the other holiday dinners, Rachel and Peter insisted on hosting the celebration at their home. They especially enjoyed the traditional sharing of New Year's resolutions and hopes and dreams of what was to come during the coming year.

Traditionally, the entire family gathered at the Stone home around 2:00 P.M. on New Year's Eve. Everyone gathered in the happy kitchen to prepare dinner together: Pizza, root beer, and vanilla ice cream. Each item was deliciously homemade—no take-out or grocery store stuff was allowed. In recent years, they had, however, given up the hand-cranked ice-cream makers and wholeheartedly welcomed the new electric kind.

The kids especially liked decorating their own pizzas once the dough had risen and had been rolled to perfection.

Pure happiness filled the Stone home. Rachel noticed that Grandpa Joe seemed a bit fidgety, but he was, nonetheless, happy. She even saw him go out onto the front porch a couple of times, and she couldn't help but wonder what he was doing. He seemed to have something sneaky up his sleeve, but when she asked him about it, he just grinned. She also noticed a twinkle in his eyes that she had not seen in a long time.

"Okay, everyone!" Peter called the family together by blowing through a shiny purple noisemaker from the table decorations. Everyone reluctantly quieted to receive their instructions. "While the pizza dough rises, and the ice-cream freezes, and the root beer . . . um . . . well . . . does whatever it does, we are going to have an igloo-building contest in the backyard." He gave them their instructions in his businesslike manner, and the children all shrieked with joy as they bolted for their winter wear. They retrieved their clothing and then listened carefully as they dressed themselves.

"Each family is to construct an igloo. You will have exactly ninety minutes to finish. You will make them as imaginative as possible. Grandpa Joe will be with Wally and Angela's family. Ready? Go."

"Wait, wait, wait," Paul interrupted and stopped everyone before they reached the door. "How come I can't be with Grandpa?"

The other children echoed Paul.

"Okay, okay," Peter relented. "Grandpa and the kids will build one igloo. The women will build one, and the men will build the best one. How's that sound?"

"Yahoo!" Grandpa and the children screamed. "But ours will be the best," Sara called on her way out. Rachel, Angela, and Christina argued that theirs would definitely be the most creative.

But the men, already on the porch, yelled that they would definitely be finished first.

* * *

"*I know Dad invited us, Annie, but, well . . . little Joseph is only seven days old and . . . um . . . maybe we* shouldn't take him out." Joey was, to say the least, extremely scared to rejoin his family. He knew how terribly he had hurt them, and he still blamed himself for what had happened to his mother. He understood if his family still hated him.

"Nonsense!" Annie was thrilled to get to meet Joey's family and to have them meet their son. "If they are all as great as your father, then this will be wonderful!"

"But Dad wasn't always like he is now. He used to be very unemotional. And Christina told me she hated me . . . And Angela's husband, Wally . . . he's a shrink. What if he tries to analyze me? And, well . . . I just . . ."

"Oh, so what you're saying, dear husband of mine, is that it's not possible for people to change?"

Joey knew immediately how right she was. He closed his eyes and took a deep breath. "You're right, Annie." He opened his eyes and smiled at her. "You're always right. I, of all people, know that people can and do change."

"Yes, we do."

So they loaded the baby into the car and headed for the Stone residence. Annie reassured Joey the whole time they drove. Finally, they arrived.

"It's only six P.M., Annie. He said dinner would be at six thirty. Should we drive around for a while?" Joey's hands were sweating and his mouth was dry.

"He also said to come at two P.M. for fun and games. I think we're okay to go in now."

"But . . ." Joey tried to stall, but Annie was already undoing baby Joseph's car-seat straps. She handed Joey the diaper bag and carefully lifted the baby out.

"Come around to my door and I'll hand him to you so you can carry your son in to meet your family."

* * *

The paper plates were artistically arranged on the New Year's Eve table. The centerpiece was made of ribbons and balloons and noisemakers and hats—in every color imaginable. Each paper plate was a different, shimmery color, with cups and utensils to match. "Happy New Year" banners cut out of colored foil letters dangled from several strings placed around the big dining room. The excited family began to seat themselves and get ready for the blessing.

"Everyone sit wherever you'd like," Peter called out above the noisy children. Of course, they all raced to sit beside Grandpa Joe, who kept checking his watch and glancing toward the big windows. Rachel remembered that he was up to something.

"What is it, Dad? Are you expecting someone?" she teased.

"Me? . . . Oh . . . I just noticed that we're eating twenty minutes early. It's only six ten. You said dinner was at six thirty."

"And does that matter?" Rachel egged him on.

"No . . . I . . . guess not. I mean, I guess no one minds." Grandpa Joe looked around the table. He was beginning to believe that Joey wasn't coming, and he couldn't really blame him.

Everyone found a chair, and Christina beamed at Angela. Finally, there were no extra places set and no extra chairs.

Rachel had exercised the greatest self-control she could muster. She wanted to start off the New Year right, by making everyone happy. Besides, since she had explained everything to everyone, she didn't feel such a need to set the extra place. In addition to that, Joey had called to tell her about the baby, so she knew they wouldn't be coming. Joey, of course, had not mentioned his New Year's invitation and his reunion with Joseph since Joseph had wanted it to be a surprise.

Annie bravely led Joey to the front steps, where she quickly rang the doorbell. She turned, took Joey's arm, and stood by his side waiting and wondering. She breathed deeply and looked at her husband and son.

Joey cradled little Joseph securely in his arms and thought how very blessed he was. Though he was painfully aware of all he had lost, he was filled with joy at what he had been able to recover. He had found what really mattered in life. His wife and his son were truly a new beginning, and God was offering him another chance. He marveled that God would allow him to be a part of Annie and Joseph's lives—they were so good, so pure. Gratitude overcame him as they stood waiting for the door to open. Joey finally believed that he truly belonged. He finally saw that God, in His love and wisdom, had always offered him a place to fit in . . . a family to love him and to be loved by him. Why hadn't he seen it before? Finally, he could return to them and offer himself completely.

He felt tears pooling in his eyes, and when he tried to blink them away, they dropped like rain onto little Joseph's soft, blue blanket. Try as he did, he couldn't stop the tears from falling. Annie looked at him and felt his gratitude. She couldn't wait for them all to be a family.

Slowly the door opened. Rachel held out her arms.

"Joey," she whispered through her tears. He handed her his precious bundle. "Annie." Rachel held them all in her outstretched arms. "You came. Oh . . . finally, you came."

* * *

When the doorbell rang and Rachel left to answer it, Grandpa Joe knowingly bounded to the kitchen. He frantically grabbed two extra place settings from the bar next to the sink and rushed back to the dining room table.

"Quick!" he called. "Everyone make room!" The puzzled family just stared at Grandpa Joe. "Stand up, everyone . . . move down, hurry. We've got to set two more places. Angela, two chairs, quick."

Still the family sat and stared.

"What is wrong with you people? Rachel has set an extra place the past two years, and now you question me? Please, just DO IT!"

Reluctantly, everyone made room for two extra places. Grandpa Joe threw the place settings on the table and rushed back to his own place. Angela and Wally each retrieved an extra chair. Everyone sat in silence. Rachel entered first, smiling at her father. She immediately nodded her approval at the extra places. Then she stepped aside to allow Annie, Joey, and baby Joseph to be seen.

Christina nearly knocked over her chair trying to reach her brother and his family. And everyone else followed suit. What a beautiful reunion. Joey had returned and the family was together once again. God answered their prayers, and Rachel's childhood belief that families are always together for the holidays became a reality.

Rachel moved to Peter and held him close to her. He had many questions, as they all did, but Rachel insisted that they all sit down and begin their New Year's Eve meal before answering questions.

After the prayer, Joseph Keller Sr. raised his plastic cup of homemade root beer and vanilla ice cream. "To our family!" he toasted. "May we never stop hoping."

Epilogue

Sitting in Dad's leather chair, I can see them drive up in Joey's new white Ford truck. He still enjoys a powerful truck. His curly blond hair has turned mostly white, still unruly—but a nice shade of gray. And he certainly doesn't move as fast as he used to. I'm glad they're here. Angela has definitely put on her share of weight in the last few years, but then we're all showing the signs of our age. Even Christina moves more slowly; the arthritis in her back gives her such fits.

Through the trees I can see them making their way up the front walk, and I can't help but chuckle to think that no one escapes time's remodeling clutches.

I'm excited to spend some time with them even though it's not easy to say good-bye to all of Mom and Dad's stuff. They'll be as touched as I am that Dad chose to use red gloves instead of a will. Dad knew that the gloves would serve two purposes: the obvious, legal aspect, of course, is to divvy out his belongings, but the more important and sentimental role that the gloves play is to remind each of us of our long-past Christmas journey, the miracle of repentance, and the hope we can all find in Christ.

I'm sure Dad knew that the gloves would inspire us to sit down on more than one occasion and recount the events of that glorious holiday season—Santa's visit, our miraculous journey, our incredible star, the birth of Joseph Jr., and, finally, our New Year's reunion. By the way, I finally remembered how I knew Santa. He was Joey's kind-hearted drug court judge. I knew I recognized his handsome blue eyes . . . and the accent was, of course, an act. Apparently, he and his sons all dress as Santa every year. They gather Christmas for those who need it most. Judge John Christianson is his name—I had to do some real detective work to figure that one out. We are so blessed to have made our way onto their Santa list that year.

We will continue to laugh and cry over the dear memory every time we gather, and each time we share our story, it will remind us of another Christmas Eve journey so long ago. We will continue to recall the wise men who studied the heavens and followed a new star to Bethlehem, and, most significantly, we will never forget that like the North Star, the Atonement of Jesus Christ will always be here heralding hope, offering forgiveness, and promising peace. What a miracle!

About the Authors

Husband and wife duo Larry and Lisa Laycock have been teaming up on joint creative projects for the past 25 years. In 1995, the Laycocks created their first book, *Gathering Christmas,* sharing their belief that small acts of kindness can touch hearts and change lives forever. In 1996, the Laycocks introduced a sequel to *Gathering Christmas* titled *Evergreen Miracles.* After initial release of the two books, *Gathering Christmas* and *Evergreen Miracles* sold over 250,000 copies.

In 1993 Larry and Lisa wrote and produced a musical production named *Joshua. Joshua* has enjoyed success in the western United States.

Larry, currently a senior shareholder with the law firm of Workman Nydegger is an experienced trial attorney specializing in intellectual property litigation. He was recently recognized as one of the "Best in the U.S." in his field of specialty and helped to earn his firm's recognition as one of the top intellectual property law firms in the United States.

Lisa, a writer, poet, and lyricist, earned a Bachelor of Arts Degree in English Education from Brigham Young University. She retired early from teaching high school English and coaching dance to be with their children.

The Laycocks are the parents of four children and live in Alpine, Utah.